# The 716
# Back to
# BUSINESS

# Table of Contents

# Acknowledgement

First I would like to thank everyone for showing me love and reading The 716 Love & Consequences. I know that it was my first published work, so I appreciate your patience as I worked through a few issues that inspired me to be better and do better. So thank you for overlooking the grammatical errors in the first book and focusing on the story. You'll be happy to know that through this learning process, I have grown and made the needed adjustments to make sure the story stays the focus. I am committed to delivering an exceptional product each and every time, one that I can be proud of but most importantly one you will be inspired to read. My hope is that through my stories, we see life differently, view love more honestly and embrace all that is unique about each other. So Thank you for allowing me to share a piece of my world with you.

I would like to thank my Publisher, D & S Publishing. It was out of your frustration that you formed a great company that is assisting authors like myself and providing opportunities to be guided through the process. You continue to show me the value in partnerships and why certain elements are important to the success of your book. I appreciate all of your hard work and your attention to detail in assisting me to create a professional product.You truly are making Publishing Simple.

To all my girlfriends that laugh, cry, hold each other up, that build up each other and instill confidence in one another, you are the soul reason why we rock! These characters reflect some of the best qualities in friendship. Where would any of us be without the love and support of our sisterhood. Nekeisha, Natasha, Lanita, CeCe, Trish, Trinka, Amina, Ashanti, Ayanna, Tevon, Rose, Liz, Deana, and Evette, you give me life, a shoulder to cry on, a listening ear countless moments of laughter, not to mention all the memories I hold dear. Thank you for being my support no matter how near or far or the time in between.

To my family, thank you for your undying support. Your feedback, your encouragement and patience means the world to me. To my sons who the moment you find out I was in the middle of writing a chapter, quickly got of the phone with me and told me to finish up and get it done, thank you for allowing me to take time away from you to do something for myself. Your unselfishness inspires me to give more and love harder.

To my husband who without a doubt is the air I breathe, and the Sun in my universe. I watch you and see your growth and determination and you inspire me to just be great. People ask me who is the character Que modeled after and I always grin and remember 1990 and us growing up. I have loved you since the beginning and before I even know how good this love could be. We have fought through all the odds and proved many wrong. Through trial and error, we have become masters of our own world and have proven that love can conquer all. You are the dopest representation, unapologetically beYoutiful, the coolest, calmest and bravest Black Man I know. Your smile provides the shade I long for during long summer days and the warmth I need to survive a winter vortex. It melts me and builds me up and that makes you the only mutherfucka I need in my corner! Thank you for All you give to me especially when I know what I ask of you some days requires you giving a little more.

Lastly to the musicians of the 1990's that sung the songs, wrote the lyrics and laid the hottest beast that still have us jammin to this day, you inspired this story. It is a pleasure to walk down memory lane listening to your creative geniuses. Your songs were the backdrop to so many great memories and events. Thank you for creating the playlist to our lives.

# "What A Fool Believes"

**- Doobie Brothers**

**Anika**

I can't believe that this is my life. In just a few weeks my baby will be born. This baby will be so loved. Aaron and I will be getting married soon and starting our lives as husband and wife. I have a big beautiful new home to decorate and all the money a girl from E. Ferry and Humboldt could imagine. My life is almost perfect. Almost, I think to myself as I stroll through the grocery store. I loved shopping at Wegmans. Everything was always so fresh and clean. And, if I went at the right time during the day, I could beat the afternoon rush.

I walk through the store smiling, thinking of my wonderful life. I always thought I would make a great mother and wife; I just imagined it differently. Most girls would give anything to be in my shoes… shit, I won't complain. If you can't have what you want, take what you need. And that is exactly what I'm doing, looking out for me and mines. I was going to make this work; I thought to grab some fresh plums and peaches. After all, I was happy. Or as happy as I could be.

That's strange. I could have sworn I grabbed a package of salmon. Oh well, I'll grab another package I thought, as I headed over to the meat counter. The guy behind the counter smiled and greeted me kindly.

"I'll take 2 T-bone steaks, 2 Porterhouses and 2lbs of ground beef" I stated completing my order. I rubbed my belly awaiting the neatly wrapped meat packages.

I have to admit, for being 8 months pregnant I was still the envy of women. My baby bumps help to accentuate my small waist even more. All my curves were more defined. But my breast was off the hook. I carried the perky 38DD's as if they had always been attached to me. I wanted to make sure that I kept myself up during this pregnancy. I know they say you should be eating for 2, which I did, within reason. But I would not get carried away. I had to keep my man still interested. My girlish figure was still on point. Fuck maternity clothing, I could still fit into regular sized clothing, so I just went up a size, and all was good.

"Is there anything else I can get for you, pretty lady" the meat attendant asked as he walked around the counter and placed my packages in my cart.

I smiled and answered, "No, but thank you."

I walked away and could tell that he and the 2 men who were behind me in line at the meat counter eyes followed my hips as they swayed and switched me away to my next grocery list item. I giggled knowing that I still had my power and the excitement I could cause.

I made my way to the checkout line after spending about 45 minutes walking up and down the aisles. As I started placing my groceries on the conveyor belt, I got a weird feeling. Chills ran up and down me like a brisk breeze just ran through the store targeting me. I looked around and did not notice anyone or thing that seemed out of place. That was strange I thought. Those days are long gone; there couldn't possibly be any reason for me to be looking over my shoulder. Besides life is good; damn near perfect. The grocery bagger placed my groceries in the cart and asked which way I was park. I lead the way, and he followed. I love the perks that came with being pregnant. All the extra attention and help was always welcome. I unlocked the car and in went the bags.

"Thank you so much for helping me" I gestured

"No problem Anika" he replied walking away in the opposite direction from the store.

# "Back to Life"

### - Soul ll Soul.

**Yazz**

It felt good to be back in Ruff Buff. It has been almost 9 months. Don't get me wrong I loved being with Jay. This whole ordeal has brought us closer, but there is nothing like home. Buffalo has some of the best food in the country. But before I pig out, I need to see my girls. A Bitch gone has some explaining to do. I told Jay I would meet him at the new house later on. I knew he had business to attend to and if there is anything I learned over the past few months, business needs to be handled first and foremost. Being that close to him gave me a whole new understanding of the game. I've done things and saw things that I can honestly say I thought I would never. It's made me stronger and harder; I'm no longer timid or scared. The naive I left the minute we rode into Michigan; the minute I fired my first shot; the minute I said yes to Jay and his way of life. Ya girl was back, just a different version than before.

I had the all clear from Jay and Que to venture out. I spent 3 weeks cooped up in our new house. It was away from the streets of Buffalo. Clarence, NY is no place for Blacks. It was, however, the perfect escape from the hard life we lived and a chance to forget the world we were held captive too. There was only so much decorating one person could do. As far as I was concerned the house was perfect. The house set back on 5 acres of land. Jay had a security gate and station placed at the beginning of the driveway. The house set back almost an acre. There was no way anyone was getting onto the property without being invited or seen. Our closest neighbors were cows and corn fields. We were out here, in our little piece of serenity. The house has 5 bedrooms and 4 baths. The basement was turned into a game room complete with a billiard, poker and game table. Centipede and Mrs. Pacman arcade systems adorned the corners of the room. Jay's office was also located down there. Yep, life was good if you looked at the money and other material things that we acquired. I just hope Jay keeps his promise; then life would be complete.

# "Funkdafied"

**- Da Brat**

## Monica

"**D**amn!" I yelled, "This shit is the real real!" I uttered taking a puff of the la and passing it back to Mario. He puffed as I inhaled his dick into my mouth. I stroked him as if he was the Chronic that got me high. I sucked and watched his body squirm, and he moaned with excitement. I got his dick hard enough for me to mount him again and I rode my way into the evening. Mario was blessed. His piece was not only thick but long as hell. This young dude had me on ten, and he knew what to do with it too. He had a bitch wanting to settle down and do the wifey thang when he took it from the back. He rode this pussy like a cowboy wrangling in the cattle. Every time he thrust into me, my ass would shake, and I rode that wave like a surfer. Plus, this nigga had stamina!! We would pull all-nighters!! I rode him until he took every last drop of my juice and he exploded inside me.

Now don't get me wrong, what Mario and I did was pure business. Since Que and Jay left, someone had to make sure Mario was safe. Que told me to look after him, so I did. I'm always the first to hear of shit on these streets. I report to him just like I did Que minus the sex. If Mario ever needed anything, he knew I had his back, and in return, he would take care of me. It did not matter one fuck if he got a girl. I know my place, and he knows his. And anytime one of us just need to chill and relax we know where to find each other. Besides, let him tell it, my pussy better than hers anyway. And she doesn't give HEAD! It's just a matter of time before he let that chick go.

Mario let me know that Que and Jay were back. It had been almost 9 months since all hell broke loose and the family was split into different directions. First with the death of Ayanna, and then without so much as a whisper Que, Jay and Yazz disappeared. Anika cried for days. Shit, even I was fucked up over that shit. I knew there had to be a good reason; it was just the timing was all wrong. We needed them; Anika needed Que. It's good that everyone is ok, and we can finally get the gang back together. All I know is somebody better tell Anika that Que is back. Her wedding is in 2 months, and the baby is due in less than that. Hell, I wonder if Que knows. Just thinking about that shit is killing my buzz.

# "NY State of Mind"

**- Nas**

**Que**

Jay and I sat at the middle of the antique mahogany table. We were surrounded by the heads of the family. I answered the questions they posed. I was honest. I gave graphic details, numbers, and names. Uncle Clio nodded with approval. Auntie Willa gave her blessing, and the others followed. Jay presented each of the 9 members at the table with a perfectly wrapped box. Inside was a token of our undying gratitude to the family. I had customized Rolexes made for each member. After everyone opened the box and accepted their gift, I spoke.

"Thank you all for your faith and trust in me. Everything that I do and has done has been to preserve our family's name and way of life. I will continue to uphold the family name; I will continue to expand the territory; I will continue to dominate our adversaries and extinguish those that stand against us. I am forever in your debt, and I will not let you down" I stood there as I addressed them looking them each in their eyes.

"As a token of my gratitude, please accept my gifts of love. You will also find a suitcase filled with one million each in your cars. This symbolizes the continued fortune of the family."

They whispered with approval. Jay sat calmly at the table. He was confident, and so was I. We knew this was our turn and a chance to take the business to new heights. Plus, this was the only way either of us was going to be able to leave the game one day. We needed to get off the streets and focus on the inner workings of the family. Control the game from behind the closed doors. More importantly, be able to have the lives we both wanted with the women we loved.

They clapped with approval. Uncle Big L offered up a toast. We drank the shot of Cognac one after another until everyone had blessed us with a toast. It had been done. I was the head of the family with Jay as my right-hand man. There was still business to be had. We needed to meet with the different sects of the family. Restructure some things; plan and get organized. Jay was taking care of that along with Uncle Clio. They would announce the family meeting to be held 2 days from today. This would give everyone time to make arrangements to be present. We will call it a family reunion of sorts. Everything was already paid for. Attendance was not optional; I could not wait. In 2 days

I could walk the streets again, this time as the head of the most powerful family in the state. But in 2 days I was going to get my woman, Anika. In 2 days all would be right again.

# "Flava in Ya Ear-Remix"

**- Craig Mack**

**Jay**

Que and I sat in VIP as we watched everyone from Lieutenants to Sergeants, Capos, to Majors walk through the doors to pay their respects as they were summoned by the family. Mario was now the new us on the streets. He was the Top General appointed by Que. All territories reported to Mario now. Mario had his eyes and ears on everything. He was the only one allowed from this point on to address Que and me. If there was an issue of any kind, Mario was the first to know and was given authority to act to resolve said issue. Mario was being groomed as was Que and I to one day sit at the head of the family. We watched as dudes from up and down the eastern coast presented their gifts as Mario greeted them one by one. I had only sat through one of this changing of the guard ceremonies. With any luck, this would be

My last passing of the sword before I retired.

Mario called the meeting to order. There must have been about 400 dudes seated according to position and region. The heads of the family were all present as well as Uncle Sarge. Uncle Sarge was retiring, hence the passing of the sword. He was dressed in a black custom made suite that was adorned with gold buttons and a pair of black and gold wingtip gates. He stood a very proud and hardened man. He had been in the game since we were youngins, if not before that. When Uncle Sarge spoke which we all knew was not that often, we knew he meant business. Uncle Sarge took the stage. He spoke of the direction of his reign and how the family grew to be the dominant force under his watch. He talked about the many lives that were lost and their impact on his heart and to the family. He announced his retirement with the smoothness of a shot of whiskey. Many of us only knew of Uncle Serge's rein. For many of us being born into the family or growing up with the family, he was the dominant face of this empire. He was all we knew. His announcement came as a shock to many; all but the select few.

Auntie Willa took the stage next. No one in the family was more feared than Auntie Willa. Willa Mae was born the only girl of 11 siblings. She was the epitome of rough and ready. Even in her ripe old age, the very sight of her made grown ass men cower. There are stories of her and her ruthlessness. All I know was she was the Matriarch of the family, and if she ever had to come to see or call for you, it was never a good thing. Few have ever been seen or heard from again after she summoned them. With dead silence in the room, Auntie Willa spoke. She announced that Que would be heading up the family as the Father. She proceeded to announce that I was the right hand of the father and that Uncle Clio had been assigned, Concierge. Mario is the Head General as appointed by Que. With these few words Aunt Willa gave her blessings, and by a show of hands from the heads of the family empire the new reign was approved publicly and blessed. The room erupted in applause as Que stood and was greeted by the heads of the family. Mario took the stage and announced for the festivities to begin

It was a celebration to top all celebrations. The family spared no expense. Liquor flowed like rivers, and a sea of fine ass women emerged on us like a flood. There were food and every delicacy that would delight even the pickiest of eaters. They flew in two of the hottest DJ's from NYC. They kept the party hype, and the dance floor packed. People walked by the VIP sending their congrats and well wishes. Niggas were showering us with all kinds of gaudy ass gifts. We had bottles of Cristal being brought to VIP by the dozens; it was amazing. Que just sat there watching and enjoying the atmosphere. It was well deserved. Que had done his time, and more importantly, he hadn't even asked for this. The Family just appointed him. It was the beginning of what would soon be our end; or the rest of our lives.

# "I Never Wanna Live Without You"

**- Mary J Blige**

**Anika**

I arrived home to find the sweetest handwritten note on the kitchen counter. It told me to get dressed and that there would be a car arriving at 6:30 to pick me up. There was a white box with a big red ribbon on the bed. The card read I can't wait to see you tonight. Inside was a red lace dress with off the shoulder straps. The lining in the dress was a nude color, and the lace offered some stretch. Which was a good thing as my stomach seem to be growing daily. Beside that box was another smaller white box, again wrapped with a red bow. Inside was the perfect pair of strappy gold sandals. I giggled.

"This man sure knows how to spoil me." I thought out loud.

I quickly took a shower and got ready for my date. I wore my hair with cascading curls pinned over to one side. I went into the walk-in closet to figure out what jewelry I would be wearing only to find yet another white box. Inside was a pair of diamond teardrop earrings wrapped in gold. There was a diamond tennis bracelet that accompanied the earrings. It was beautiful. He thought of everything. I smiled. There was a note inside the box that read

"Please wear my favorite perfume and the gold clutch that matches the shoes I just bought you."

What clutch and how am I supposed to know what his favorite scent is on me? I can't recall him preferring one perfume over another. I quickly went to look in my closet for a gold clutch but instead came across a brand new clutch that sparkled like my shoes. It was just big enough for me to place my wallet, lipstick, and keys in. When I opened the purse, there was a bottle of perfume inside. I hadn't worn this is a long time. And I must admit, it was one of my favorite scents. He has one hell of a memory. The doorbell rang. I checked the cock, and it was 6:30 on the dot. I took one last look in the mirror. I looked perfect, damn near angelic. I was ready for my perfect night. I don't know what I would do without him I thought as the driver helped me into the car and we drove away.

I asked the driver if he knew our destination. All he would tell me is that it was a surprise. We rode for almost 2 hours. The tints on the windows were so dark it was hard for me to make out where we were. Just when I was getting restless and was losing my excitement and becoming hungry, I felt the car slowing down and pull up to what appeared to be a tall building. The driver quickly exited the car and walked around to open my door. I stepped out of the car only to find myself on the streets of Toronto, Canada. Wow, he went all out. With all the excitement, I didn't even notice that we crossed over a bridge or stopped at the customs station. I know we talked about going away before the baby was born, but with the Buffalo Bills making it to the Superbowl and all the after season stuff, it was hard for us to do. I guess this is the next best thing considering I can't fly this late in the pregnancy. It was beautiful. I was standing in downtown Toronto, surrounded by skyscrapers and people speaking French.

I was escorted by the doorman to the entrance to the hotel. He spoke in French. I greeted him in his native tongue. He seemed pleased at my gesture.

"Madam Anika bienvenue. J'espère que vous trouvez que vous restez agréable. Vous resterez dans le penthouse. Faites-moi savoir si vous avez besoin de quelque chose." he smiled.

"Je vous remercie. Je suis sûr que tout ira bien. J'espère profiter de votre belle ville et mon séjour ici." I replied.

I rode the elevator to the top floor. I was greeted by the doorman and the staff of the penthouse. I felt like a princess. It was all so breathtaking. Every corner of the penthouse was decorated with such style and grace. It was a setting fit for royalty, and men of the state. The view was magnificent as well. You could see the entire city from wall to wall windows that anchored the suite. I walked out onto the patio. There was a dimly lit inground pool surrounded by various seating areas. Fresh flowers accented the hardscape and blessed the air with the sweet scents of jasmine, and peonies. It was just magical.

Off in the corner was a table set for two. There was a beautiful vase with baby roses and two candles that sat in the middle of the table. I could hear the instrumental music playing in the background; he thought of everything. As I walked closer to the table, I could see the familiar white box with the red bow. The note read "to the mother of my child and the love of my life" I began to cry. I opened the box, and there was a two-carat diamond pendant necklace that hung on a thin gold necklace; it was beautiful. He had thought of everything. Every box he had given me today was so well thought out, so perfect. He knew me. It was classic and timeless and the best gesture anyone has ever done for me. I had never felt so loved and appreciated than I do at this moment. I took the necklace and tried to clasp it around my neck… I could not get the necklace to clasp. Just then I felt a familiar presence and the strength of strong masculine hands touching mine. He grabbed the necklace and clasped it closed and gently kissed my neck. At last, my prince was here.

# "You're All I Need"

**- Method Man featuring Mary J. Blige.**

**Que**

It had been eight and a half long months. I just could not wait to see Anika. There was so much I needed to tell her. And the thought that she's carrying my seed had a nigga trippin'. She may not know it, but I was there at every doctor's appointment, every ultrasound, and every outing. Maybe not in the physical, but spirit. I had a team watching her every move, just so I could make sure her, and the baby was ok. I didn't want her as much as carrying a grocery bag let alone doing any strenuous work. Had to make sure Ma and my seed were well taken care of. I have paid every last doctor bill. Sent baby gifts every time she went shopping, and someone reported that she looked at a baby item and didn't cop that. I got it for her.

I knew Anika better than she knew herself. Even when she went grocery shopping, I made sure there was nothing in the cart that would harm the baby or her. I made sure on mani-pedi days she never came out of pocket. Even when she went shopping, which she often did, I made sure my baby got everything she wanted and deserved. That punk ass nigga Aaron stood bye as he paid for shit. He knew I pulled trump every single time. I also told his lame ass I would be back for her. Well, I'm back. And Anika is mined, and that baby too. Nothing is going to stop me from getting what's mine.

I arrived at the hotel in Toronto, Canada. I was informed that Anika had arrived just 10 minutes prior, had a nigga feeling butterflies and shit. Anika always did have that effect on me. I rode the elevator to the penthouse suite. She did not hear me enter; she was mesmerized by the beautiful layout of the suite. She looked gorgeous. She was wearing the red lace dress I purchased; I could see the diamonds in her ears sparkling in the moonlight. Neither compared to the glow she radiated. Anika took my breath away, and I could not wait to touch her and hold her in my arms.

She was opening the last gift I had for her for the night. I saw her struggling to clasp the necklace around her neck. I walked quietly over to her to assist her. I did not want to startle her and ruin the surprise. I grabbed her hands and gently took the necklace and clasped it around her neck. It felt damn good to be this close to her, I inhaled her intoxicating scent, and it was just as I remembered. I kissed her softly on her neck and back and allowed her to melt into my arms. I wrapped my arms around her and held her and our baby. I could tell she had missed my touch. I could tell, that other nigga could not hold her the way I held her. I knew at that moment Anika could find it in her heart to forgive me.

# "Freak Like Me"

### - Adina Howard

**Monica**

I was posted up on some niggas car that I met just the other day. We were making plans to fuck later on tonight when I spotted this nice ass ride turning the corner of my street. Who dis I thought to myself. If it's a nigga, you know you got to drive that. I wondered as the car got closer and I propped my ass and titties up to gain the driver's full attention. The car stopped just shy of me and the Bronco I was posted at. This nigga tryna' talk to me and I'm more interested in the car riding by. The car slowly drove up, and I turn around so that the driver could get a better full view of me. The car approached, and I was all ready for show time when the window rolled down.

"My Bitch!" I yelled as loud as I could as I watched Yazz's face appear in the window of this phat ass Alfa Romeo. I had to see for myself, as I walked over to greet her. We hugged and laughed as onlookers watched and wondered what was going on.

"Yo Monica, you went fuck me or that nigga" the dumb muthafucka in the Bronco screamed, mad that I had lost interest in his ass.

"Neither" I replied, Imma fuck the next nigga that I call, and it won't be yo dumb ass." I scolded as I turned to wave goodbye.

He drove off so fast pissed that I was no longer interested.

"I see nothin's changed" Yazz smiled as we hugged.

"You know good dick is like a metro bus, something new and good come around every 15 mins, besides all that nigga was going to get was his face in my pussy!" we laughed as I hugged her back.

"Bitch what's up?" I questioned fully of excitement.

"Hey, chica! Boy did I miss your ass" Yazz replied smiling.

"So what's up? Yall all back huh? Have you seen Anika yet?" I questioned puffing on a Philly.

"I was hoping both of yall would be together. I went by her mother's house, but no one was there. I even went by the condo where Aaron stayed, and it looked empty. So I came here. I knew your ass would be around. And from the looks of things, you up to your same shit" Yazz jokingly stated as she reached for the Philly, to my surprise.

"What the fuck! Are you smoking now? Bitch has been gone but a minute and come back all grown doing grown folks shit" I laughed as I watch Yazz hit the blunt like a pro. I continued "Damn; eight months do that kind of shit to you huh?"

"You have no fucking clue," Yazz exhaled and continued to puff.

"So tell me, how are you and Jay doing?" I asked as we leaned against the car.

"We tight. This whole experience has brought us closer together. You wouldn't believe half the shit I've done or seen this past year. All I can say is I'm happy to be back home." Yazz spoke as she zoned out thinking of the last eight months.

I could tell there was more to the story, but I wouldn't pry just yet. I was happy to have Yazz back, and for now, that would be good enough.

We rode around in Yazz's Alfa Romeo. At every stop light in every hood, niggas walked up to the car trying to get a look. They were either tryna touch the wheels or tryna holla at us. Either way, it was attention, good attention. I had a chance to fill Yazz in on Anika and the baby and Ayanna's funeral. She cried both tears of sorrow and joy.

"How could I have missed Ayanna's funeral" Yazz spoke out loud. "She was one of my closest and dearest friends."

"Look you had to do what you had to do. Shiiid… there was nothing you could do for her at that point. And I'll be damned if I would have lost another friend. So it was good yall left. Even if yall punk muthafuckas didn't say goodbye" I joked.

It made her smile.

"What about the baby? Does Que know, is it his, what about Aaron?' Yazz screamed out.

"Hold on… first yes Que knows. I told Mario to tell Que the minute I found out. Que had a whole team watchin' out for her and the baby. As far as if it's his or Aaron's I have no idea, but my money on Que. But yo, Que better makes a move soon because Anika and Aaron are set to be married in 2 months. She wanted to wait until after the baby was born. Good thing she did, or it would be the start of World War 3 knowing Que's ass" I joked

We both laughed.

We pulled up to Anika and Aaron new house. And waited at the gate to be buzzed in. There was no answer.

"So I guess Aaron is taking real good care of Anika?" Yazz questioned.

"Yeah, but there is something about this nigga… I just can't place it but something about him ain't right. Almost like he too good" I commented hesitantly.

"Well we back now, and if Que has his way, Aaron will be out of the picture soon anyway" Yazz chimed in. "Besides, if he is no good or hiding something between you and I we'll find out," she said confidently as we high fived each other and pulled out of the driveway

# "Mc's Act Like They Don't Know"

**- KRS One**

**Jay**

I got off the phone with Que. He was getting ready to make his move with Anika. Better she finds out from him that he's back that from the streets. I told him to get his woman. Hell, I was going to be an uncle soon. When Que told me that shit I was in shock, almost as happy as he was. He said 100 percent proof that he knew that baby Anika was carrying was his child. That was all I needed to hear. Besides I got Que's back regardless.

I rode around in the new whip Que gave me. This Porsche was everything. It was a bit flashy for my taste, and I would only drive it on special occasions, but a brother had to take it for a spin. I cruised the streets of Buffalo on a natural high.

Listening to Babyface "Whip Appeal" had me feeling some kinda way. Like maybe Yazz and I should start a family of our own, or maybe I should stop bullshittin' and ask her to marry me. Either way, I knew how Yazz felt about the lifestyle. She wanted me out. Hell, I wanted out. I just don't think she would be ready for the next step until she knew I was done with it all. But Babyface gotcha boy is thinking. Shiiid, anything is possible at this point.

I rode as onlookers admired and gawked at my new ride. White men stared with envy and niggas nodded in approval. But one thing is for certain; everyone knew who I was. They knew. Just like a fire spreads with the blowing of the wind, news of me and Que spread like wildfire; the street was hot with the news. With the reputations we had before our temporary leave of absence, we expected there would be to no resistance. Besides, a nigga would be foolish to think they could make a move against the family, let alone me or Que at this point.

I wasn't the only one to receive such a generous gift from Que. At the end of the celebration the other night, Que gave everyone a new car. Everyone in the family that is. Lieutenants all received new Audi's, while

Sergeants took home Nissan Montero's, Capos were excited to receive brand new Alfa Romeo's and last but not least he gave Majors Ferrari's. Each car in the signature ghost grey color that represented the family and Que's rein. Mario and I walked away with top choice. I took the Porsche Carrera with the custom interior and sound system. Mario took the Mitsubishi 3000GT Spyder VR-4. The Spyder could go from 0-60 in 5.1 seconds. It was the Que also gave each warrior a duffle bag of money based on their rankings. Everyone left feeling good and excited for what Que's tenure would bring. Me, I was just cruising. And now that everyone had a chance to see me back on the streets, they knew. Without so much as a word… they knew

# "Keep Their Heads Ringin"

**-Dr. Dre**

## Mario

I just finished up business with Que and Jay. This whole week has been a blur. And now this. I guess the streets never sleep. I was waiting for the last drop of the day when my pager went off. The code entered was from Carol. Carol was a girl I met a while back. She was cool, and she knew how to keep her mouth shut. From the code I take it she wanted to see me later. We'll see about that. Just then the doorbell rang, and it was the package I was waiting for. Tommy let Kev in, and the drop was accounted for and completed. And just like the wind, Kev was gone just a quick as he appeared. I locked the package in the safe and set the security alarm. Even though the place was guarded 24/7 these were the precautions that Que put into place. It was something he had done back in Michigan to maintain security, and it worked. Que said he had learned that even the loyalist of the crew could get sticky fingers. This is why the very next day the money was moved to another location and then moved again before days end. This way the money never stayed in one location long enough for someone to be foolish enough to act. It was always under lock and key or armor patrol.

I had called Monica to see if she had plans. I know I shouldn't get involved with her, but that bitch did things to me. She had a nigga wide open. And I hate to admit it, but I preferred spending time with her than my girl. Monica was like a homie lover friend. We could be just chill and hang out, smoke a blunt or two or fuck. And sometimes do them all. Point being, she was cool people. I had been crushing on her for a while like back in the day. Now Anika is fine as hell. She had curves for days, and everyone wanted to claim that, but that was all Que, and he made it known. Yazz was like a tall goddess, but anyone could see that she and Jay had something going on even when they denied it. Ayanna rests her soul was too damn wild, but she had that exotic island look that drove men crazy.

Monica was always the less stuck up of the group, plus she nasty as hell. She had those lips, hips, and that juicy ass. Her body was cold. She was shaped like a Coke bottle, with a thirst to match. Monica was the color of peanut butter, and her hair was brown with red streaks. She stood about "5'7" and showed off every inch of her frame whenever she got the chance. When I first met the girls I was just that little sidekick. I'm all grown now and the way I make Monica scream when I hit if from the back tells me she knows that too.

So I pull up to Monica's. I told her I would be bringing a friend with me. She said coolly. Carol and I walked down the stairs into the basement. I kissed Monica and I could tell she was already lit. The music was playin', and the room smelled of Ganga. I introduced Carol to Monica. I could tell Carol was a little uncomfortable, but if she wanted to hang with me tonight; it was going to be on my terms. Besides, it's not like I made her come. Monica passes the blunt to Carol as we sit around the coffee table. She took a puff and passed it on to me.

Monica was already in the zone. And after a few more hits we all were feeling the buzz. The radio was playing in the background. One of their jams came on because both Monica and Carol started dancing. I was watching both of them interact with each other. It was hot. I sat there on the couch, rolling another blunt and watching the both shake their asses. Monica kept looking back at me with that devilish grin. I watched intensely as Monica moved her hips and body to the beat of the music. I could see Carol felt the competition, so she upped her game. Not to be out done, Monica came over to me and grabbed my hands and had me touching her body as she danced. Jealousy must be in the air, because Carol followed and took the blunt out of my mouth, puffed and then shook her ass on my left knee.

Monica upped the ante. She had stripped down to the matching hot pink and black thong and bra set she was wearing. She climbed the dance pole and twirled her high ass around in the most seductive manner. The look on Carol's face showed defeat. Carol watched in amazement as Monica put on a show worthy of the whole stack in my pocket. I could tell that Carol was just as turned on as I was. From the split to the upside down leg moves, the headstand, to the way she slid up and down the pole. I puffed and passed to Carol. We sat there in full awe of Monica's talents. This is why I loved spending time with her.

I applauded as Monica ended her set. She knew from the look on my face that I was dropping the paper on her for that performance. She walked over to Carol and me. She sat on Carol's lap and took a puff of the blunt. As she exhaled she blow in Carol's face and proceeded to lock her lips with Carol. Carol kissed her back and began caressing Monica. When they came up for air, Monica's hands made their way to my pants and unzipped them. She reached in for my manhood. I was already erect from the dance routine she had performed, I had to pull my jeans down and allow her to continue. She grabbed my dick and began to suck up and down my shaft. She sucked and took me down her throat as if I was a long medical instrument searching her tonsils. Monica took Carol's hands and placed them on her pussy. Carol stroked Monica's pussy. I could hear the juice from Monica getting wetter and wetter with each stroke from Carol. Monica then invited Carol to join her by removing her hands from her wet pussy and having Carol massage the juice onto my hard dick. Carol stroked my shaft as Monica sucked my head. Then Carol followed Monica's lead, and they both began sucking up and down the sides of my shaft. Up and down they went as I screamed and moaned. It took all I had not to bust a nut.

I pulled away and pulled my jeans completely off. Monica was helping Carol undress. And then we gathered on the couch. Monica was laying there as Carol began to lick her pussy. My eyes were wide open in shock. I had no idea Carol was down for a 3way let alone licking pussy. But Monica had a way of making anyone do things they normally would not do. She was licking Monica's clit as I was entering Carol from the back. I fucked Carol as Carol enjoyed Monica. The music played in the background, and our high was in full effect. With each stroke I gave Carol, she shook and buried her head deeper into Monica, and she would moan.

We then switched. I laid there on the coach as Monica rode my dick like a champ and Carol sat on my face as my tongue entered into her warm soul. I could hear Monica and Carol kissing as I satisfied them both. We fucked and fucked until our bodies became a sticky mass of brown and chocolate melanin. I took a breather as Monica fucked Carol with her strap on dildo. She had Carol on all fours and then with her legs in the air. All I saw was Carol being worn out like nothing I had done before. I was almost jealous. Not at two chicks fucking, but there was Monica enjoying someone other than me. I quickly joined in. This time I went after Monica. I took her from the back doggy style and entered her with the vengeance of a god at war. I fucked her hard. Every inch of my thirteen and a half inch dick went deep into her. I could feel the walls of her pussy releasing hot lava as she screamed out in pleasure. I took her pussy as if I was trolling for a buried treasure. Monica came and came all over my dick, and I loved it. I loved that I satisfied her this way. And when I was done pleasing her pussy, I entered her ass. I stroked her gently; touching her face as she sucked my fingers. I grabbed her hair and forced all of me into her as she came. She shook her ass on my dick, and it drove me crazy. She rode that dick back while I stroked her tight ass. It was the best feeling, not even my girlfriend had allowed me to enjoy her like this, but Monica was down. She allowed me to explore her and please her. Monica then climbed on top of me as we sat on the edge of the couch and she rode me. Up and down, up and down went her rodeo. Her legs wrapped around me and me pulling on her wet hair and holding her back to push her deeper into me. Monica rode me until we both climaxed. We ended both letting out long sighs and moans of accomplishments.

Carol was passed out on the other end of the couch. Monica lit another blunt and then started talking about basketball. She asked me about what was going on If there was anything she could help me with? How fuckin' cool was this. Monica was a down ass bitch that I could easily catch feelings for. Even when I knew I know better. But she just fucked me and my side chick, now tell me that ain't every man's dream girl.

# "Love Don't Live Here Anymore"

- **Faith Evans**

**Anika**

"YOU HAVE GOT TO BE FUCKIN' KIDDING ME RIGHT?" I yelling at the top of my lungs. "What makes you think you can just walk back into my life and think everything is going to be ok? You've got some nerve" I spoke up holding onto my belly as tears streamed down my face.

"Anika, listen… I know I hurt you, I didn't have a choice…" Que spoke as I cut him off.

"You had a choice, you could have stayed, or better yet you could have taken me with you" I yelled over him.

"You know I could not do that baby. I couldn't put you in harm's way again. And now with you having our baby, I just could not imagine putting both of you in harm's way." Que continued.

"Baby! Baby! You don't honestly think that this baby is yours, do you?" I argued. "Aaron and I are having a baby, so don't you worry about me and this baby" I cried.

"Anika, I know that baby is mine, and so do you. You can be mad at me all you want, but that baby is mine. Not you or that nigga Aaron is going to stop me from taking care of my seed" Que said sternly as he stared me in my eyes.

His eyes were intense; his facial expression was hard. I knew that he meant every word that he had spoken.

"You left me! You abandoned what we had. I loved you, and I thought you loved me. Do you know how that felt? I waited and waited, but you never came home. I stayed in that house for weeks waiting, worried and scared that something had happened to you. I cried myself to sleep every night. I had to hear it from Mario that you were gone. I begged like some random chick for information about you, anything. Where were you at, were you ok and he gave me nothing. My heart broke. All I wanted was for you to come back to me. No calls, no letters, no nothing. Do you have any idea how that feels? I loved you; you made me promises that you knew that you could not keep. I have musta been a fool to believe that you would ever put me first. All those years I spent wishing and hoping that you'd notice me and love me. I used to dream of you and me. You put that in my heart. And then we finally get to that place, and you leave. You ran. You never said goodbye; you just left me. I can't do this with you anymore. You hurt me, you broke my heart, and now you want to act as nothing has happened. I needed you, and you were nowhere to be found. I can't feel that way again. I can't allow you to do that to me again. I can't allow you to think that what you did to me is ok. You said that you loved me. I cried and cried. All that pain I felt that my heart ached, those thoughts of you...bad things happening to you, do you have any idea what that was like for me? You don't do this to someone you love Que; love isn't supposed to hurt. You hurt me bad. I felt like I was losing my mind without you, I couldn't breathe, and now you're here. Like everything is ok. It's not ok!! None of what you put me through is ok! And I don't give a damn what you say, Que, whatever you have to say, it's eight months, two weeks, three days and twelve hours too late!" I cried as tears rolled continuously down my face.

I walked away from Que holding my stomach. All that pain and hurt came rushing back again. It was too much, coupled with the fact that I had not eaten anything since earlier today, the dizziness set in. All I knew was that everything went dark.

# "I Can't Sleep"

### - R. Kelly

**Que**

"ANIKA!" I screamed as I ran to her side catching her before she fell to the floor. I yelled for someone to call an ambulance or doctor. The staff of the penthouse came running in to assist me while the door man ran to the elevator to wait for the hotels on-call physician to arrive. I sat there holding her in my arms.

"Can the doctor hurry the fuck up" I yelled in frustration as the minutes seemed like hours.

"Anika, I got you, baby, everything is going to be ok. I'm so sorry, I'm so sorry baby" I whispered holding her for dear life. What have I done I thought. All this pressure, pain and hurt. She had to be ok. The baby had to be ok I thought to myself. Just then I heard the elevator doors open, and a slender older gentleman approached. He rushed in got down on his knees and immediately listened for her heartbeat and then the baby's heartbeat. He had me carry Anika into the bedroom so that he could examine her. He closed the door behind him only after making sure that everyone including myself was out.

The doctor and his staff emerged finally after 20 mins alone with Anika.

"Doctor, is she gonna be ok?" I asked

"She's dehydrated, and she needs her rest. No stress. With her being so late in her pregnancy, any unnecessary stress would not be good for her or the baby. I have her hooked up to an IV with a saline solution to get some fluids into her. I'll be back tomorrow afternoon to check on her. Until then let her get some rest. Your wife needs her rest." the doctor spoke in English with a thick French accent.

"Thank you, doctor. I'll take good care of her and the baby." I replied

I was relieved by the diagnosis. Upset that I caused this stress, but relieved that Anika and the baby were ok. We shook hands as I walked the doctor to the elevator doors and spoke our goodbyes. I rushed back to be by Anika's side. She lay there angelic like. Peaceful. All I wanted to do was be with her. I did not mean for this to happen. All the things I wanted to tell her. Me coming home. Us being here in this moment was all because I loved her. How am I ever gonna make this up to her? How am I gonna get her to trust me again? I just want to be with her. Nothing else matters, except her and our baby. I just need her to know this. I'm not going nowhere until she knows this.

I sat there at her bedside watching and waiting. I rubbed her belly and held her hand. She would moan from time to time when I touched her belly; it was a sound of approval. I could feel the baby moving, and every once in a while there would be a kick from the baby to let me know he/she knew I was there. It brought tears to my eyes. Finally being able to be here, to finally be able to see her, to feel our baby moving. After all these months of watching from afar. I was here, and this is not at all how I pictured it. I made many promises in the past, but this one was one I would bet my name on. From this day forward it would be about Anika and my child. I vowed that I would always be here for them. Nothing was more important than them. And watching her lay here like this made it all so clear to me.

# "Can't You See"

**- Total**

## Anika

It must have been a dream. I would be a fool to believe Ques was back; I thought as I lay there in bed. I could feel the warmth and familiar hands of love around me. It felt good to be held.  I would pretend even if I knew it was not Que. I lay there wishing. My head felt dizzy, and before long I feel back to sleep.

I woke up to unfamiliar surroundings. It took me a moment to put everything together; my memory escaped me. I felt like I had slept for days. I was so relaxed and rested. As I began to regain my bearings, it became clear. Oh my goodness… "QUE" I screamed out loud.

Rushing into the bedroom was Que followed by what looked like a nurse and doctor.

"Anika everything is going to be ok. Calm down baby" I heard Que say.

"Ah, Madame Anika. Vous avez finalement réveillé. Tu nous a fait peur. Reste calme. Nous devons nous assurer que le bébé va bien ok." the gentlemen spoke.

I watched as he took a few vitals. He wrapped the blood pressure cuff on my arm. He took my results and wrote them down as the nurse adjusted the IV drip that I had not noticed was connected to my right hand. I was confused.

"What happen Que?" I asked puzzled.

"Anika, you fainted and scared the shit out of me. The doctor came to check on you again. You've been going in and out for a few days now. We just needed to make sure you and the baby were ok." Que commented.

"A few days! What day is it?" I began to panic with concern.

"Calm down Ms. Anika, this excitement is not good for you and the baby" the doctor spoke as he touched my hand taking a quick pulse check. "You need to rest" he added. "I'll return tomorrow, and we can talk about you leaving then." He finished as he shook Que's hand and exited the bedroom.

Que stood there staring at me. His eyes hung heavy, and there was a look of solace on his face. I can't believe that he is here. I thought I had dreamt him here, but no, he was here. I had waited eight months for this moment, and now I had no words. He stared.

"Que. I was interrupted

## Que

"Anika... you don't need to say anything. Everything you said the other night was true, I let you down. I made promises that I did not keep. I'm so sorry that I hurt you. I'm so sorry that I put you through all of this. I don't know if you'll ever forgive me, I don't know if you should. All I wanted to do was love you... I just wanted to show you... I just wanted to come home to you. I never meant to put you and our baby in harm's way. How selfish of me to think that I could just waltz back in here and everything would be ok. But for eight months, two weeks, and some days, all I could think about was you and our baby. There was not a day that went by that I did not know what you were doing. Every doctor's appointment, every ultrasound, every outing you took, I knew about. I know that sounds crazy, but it was the only way I could be a part of your life. I needed to know that you were ok. That what I was putting you through by not saying goodbye did not diminish your love for me. That in some weird way you knew that I would never leave you unless it were for your protection. All I ever wanted. All I ever needed was you baby. And see what my actions have done to you. I just can't. And now I'm putting the health of our baby in jeopardy… I just .. I just .. can't." I cried kneeling on the floor confessing my sorrow and regret to Anika. At this moment is the head of the most powerful drug family in New York seemed minor compared to the power Anika had over me.

## Anika

Que laid his head into my lap as he cried in silence. He spoke from the heart. There was so much hurt in his voice. Not once did I think of what he musta been going through. I was so consumed by me and my feelings, not once did I think about Que and his feelings. I allowed him to rest on my lap. I rubbed his head following the wave pattern of his hair as we sat there in silence.

Que was home. What should be the happiest reunion has managed to cause such heartache and pain.

After about an hour of silence. Que got up and began to walk away. He was headed out of the bedroom when I spoke up "Don't go" I begged. As he turned and gave me the grin that I fell in love with.

"No worries Ma; I'm not going anywhere. I'll be right back" he guaranteed.

Que walked back into the room with the cutest and biggest stuffed Elephant. It was gray and was adorned with a polka dot black and white bow around his neck. He was perfect.

"How did you know?" I questioned.

"I told you, I was there even when you couldn't see me," Que confirmed.

"But I went back to the store to get it, and it was gone. That was over two weeks ago. You been here for 2 weeks?" I spoke getting excited.


**Que**

"Anika, calm down. We can talk, but you need to stay calm. I'll answer all your question and more, but not until you calm down." I stated authoritatively.

I continued "Yes I have been here for the last 2 weeks. There is more to the story, and we can talk about that later. I bought the elephant because I knew you wanted it. I saw the way you looked at it. When you left the store without it, I was surprised. So when you left, I went in after you and bought it. I was so disappointed. Not in you, but myself. Had I been there with you, you wouldn't even need to ask. I would have just bought that for you. Hell, I would have bought the whole damn store if you wanted. I was disappointed that you were alone carrying my baby and I was not there to hold your hand and love you the way you deserve to be loved." I spoke.

"So you watched me" Anika spoke softly trying to convince me that she was calm.

"From the day I got back, I've watched you. It was too soon for me to say anything. But the first chance I got I brought you here so that we could be alone. I just needed to have a moment with you. To talk this out with you." I answered.

Anika sat there speechless. I wasn't sure if this was good or bad thing. She was never the one who loss for words. She stared at me with those eyes. Almost as if she could read my heart and inner thoughts. She signaled for me to come closer. I hesitated at first, but I deserve whatever she was going to do. She grabbed my hand and placed it on her belly. The baby was kicking at full speed. I smiled as wide as a highway. I sat there by her side listening to and feeling all the love one person could handle. The joy brought me to be near her and enjoying this moment with her and my seed. It was more than any thug like myself deserved. But it was worth me giving up everything for including my life.

I held Anika as she slept in my arms. There were no more words spoken for the rest of the night; we were at peace. I was concerned about her and the baby 's health, anything else was irrelevant. As I promised I would tell her everything, but not tonight. Tonight, I just wanted to make sure Anika knew I would never leave her again and that my baby knew daddy was home. Yes, Daddy was home, and I would make my presence known.

# "Just to Get a Rep"

### - Gang Starr

### Aaron

"**D**amn Girl, you suck that dick like a champ," I said grinning as I walked away from her to wipe myself clean. I threw her a towel to clean herself off. I watched her as she bent over trying to wipe herself down of any evidence of the sexual acts we did. Shorty was fine as hell. She was about "5'6" with a body that mimicked one of those Victoria secret models. Her blond hair hung well down her back. She had green eyes and those pretty pink lips. Brittany was every man's dream girl. She knew how to mingle with the affluent, sophisticated crowds, had a nigga looking like a king. I never had to worry about her twisting up her lip or swinging her head right to left tryna flip on me in front of company, or when she could not get her way. She knew how to behave and never asked for anything. Hell, she picked up the tab half the time when we went out. She was my innocent good girl. Plus no matter what time a brother came home she was always ready, slippers, cigar, my drink and ready to fuck. Damn just thinking about her made my dick hard again. "Ha," I smirked.

"Oh, shit," I thought out loud. It was almost 7 pm and I hadn't spoken with Anika in three days. I keep calling the house but no answer. I musta left about ten damn messages. I gave her the number to the condo and the front office just in case something happened. With the baby's due date being so close I hated leaving her, and she couldn't come, and her spending habit won't pay for itself, so a brother had to make that money. Besides, when I'm away from home, it gives me a chance to partake in some of the privileges of being a pro athlete. Lord knows there are A LOT OF THEM! Besides, there is no way I'm going to get caught. I keep my women spread out. Never more than one honey to a town. With Anika in full mommy mode, it will be a year or two before her, and the baby can travel with me. That means daddy gets to play something other than the house. She keeps this shit up; I'll keep her ass pregnant and barefoot for 4 more years. I giggled picking up the phone to call Anika.

"Hey Anika, it's me, baby. How's my little mommy doing? I miss you and that big belly of yours. Thinking of you. Hey, listen, I'll be going out with the boys later, so hopefully, I can hear from you today. Gotta catch some footballs so that you can go shopping. Love you girl. Bye" I spoke as the answering machine beeped to conclude my message. Damn, another message. Hope mommy alright. Yeah, I'm sure she is fine. She is probably just relaxing and taking it easy. She is probably thinking about me right now. "That girl knows she makes me wanna be a better man," I said to myself. I went back into the front room to find Brittany ready for round two.

"One day I'll be the man Anika deserves, but for now, Brittany's tight ass is calling" I laughed inside grabbing on my dick and stroking it until it was met with Brittany's pretty pink lips.

"One Day," I thought, "One day."

# "Slam"

**- Onyx**

## Mario

I rode through the city checking on the crew, making sure everyone was good, keeping my ear to the streets. Heard a few things, nothing for me to worry about, but it's always good to know what the streets are talkin' bout. Had a few nigga's tryna make a name for themselves, small timers, still in diapers. We squashed that shit and made examples of their squad. Nothing was going to stand in the way of progress and money. Plus, once Que told Jay and I what happened with Anika and the baby, bothering him with this petty shit was absurd. I could handle this small stuff no problem. Jay was on top of it too. The operation of the FAM is a well-oiled, finely tuned machine. We as efficient as most fortune 500 companies and better organized than the most sophisticated associations, plus the money was better. The rate of return topped most capital gain indexes. So anybody tryna cut a slice of this pie better have a big ass knife.

I waited by the cut as the drops were made. Counted the green and made sure not a dime came up short. I had a few things to take care of before heading to Kim's. I had been neglecting her she said. So I figured I'd stop over there before heading to Monica's. Before closing up shop, I got word that one of our stash houses was just hit. I called Jay to let him know I was on it. We got a word which it was, so I was on my way. He said they would meet me there. I assumed that he was referring to him and Yazz. Ever since Yazz has been back, I've seen a different side of her; it was hot too. There was nothing hotter than a mommy who knew how to hold her own. It looked like instead of tryna change Jay into something he wasn't, Yazz finally embraced the FAM's way of life and hell, was even a soldier in her own right, which was cool for me. One more person having our back meant one fewer nigga out there tryna stab it.

I called Kim and told her I'd be there when I get there. The streets don't sleep and when they are in your streets neither do you. Me and a few of the dudes I summoned rode out to meet up with Jay. I was hoping this shit didn't take long,

besides only a crackhead would be dumb enough
to run up in our stuff like that.

# "Survival of the Fittest"

**- Mobb Deep**

**Jay**

Yazz and I rode out as soon as we got the call from Mario. Maintaining order was a must, especially with Que and Anika tied up in TO. But whoever did this wasn't mainstream. The streets were too tight. Every other corner was us. We had the block on lock, and our crew ran deep. So whoever this was, was looking for a quick fix or looking for a bullet. My money is on the first. We rode out of Clarence as I turned right onto Harris Hill Road. I refused to take the toll road when I was handling business. Those cameras caught everything and the last thing I want ever was evidence of my coming and going. I rode that down to Genesee and took the 33 Kensington all the way into the city. Yazz rubbed the back of my head and neck; it was the most relaxing feeling. It kept me calm before the storm. Her being by my side kept me focused, and calm. It was a catch 22, I loved that she was my ride or die, but you know what they say once you turn a good girl bad, she was gone forever. Yazz was well on her way to the point of no return. Michigan had taken its toll on her. There were situations and circumstances that made Yazz own up and embrace the lifestyle; It hardened her; made her cold and ruthless. It made me sad to see her innocence taken.

Headed to the westside, we rode into downtown. We had gotten word that this nigga was hiding out on some street off of Potomac Ave. We met up at the spot. Mario gave us the specs, and everyone knew their role. I was letting Mario run point on this. I was there just to make sure shit went down as planned. The last thing we needed was unwanted attention. Plus It was good for the streets to see my face from time to time. Some muthafuckas think just cause they don't see you they can pull dumb shit like this. Mario and his crew rolled out. Yazz and I stayed back and waited for the all clear. In all this heat and chaos, her presence kept me calm and cool. Yazz was the perfect complement to my hardness. She was the soft, gentle and sweet calm I needed. Although you could not tell from her outfit, she was wearing. She wore a black leather dress and black peep

Toe stilettos. Her hair was pulled back in a ponytail with curls. She was my around the way girl. She had big gold hoop earrings that dangle and framed her face and gold bangles draped her right arm. She was fierce and ready. I knew somewhere on her, underneath that skin-tight dress and above those stilettos and legs, she was packin'. And that was more of a turn on than anything.

It only took about 15 mins before the call came in. Mario had paged me the all clear code, and we rode in. I pulled up to the house and opened the car door for Yazz. We walked in like the joint was ours, at this moment it was. It was a goddamn shame. This place was as nasty as one could imagine. Roach infested and crying babies everywhere. This shit was ridiculous. A house full of crackheads basin off the shit they stole from us. Shawn, one of Mario boys, gathered the kids up and took them into the back of the house. I was ruthless but humane. Ain't no way I wanted the kids to be around for what happened next. Mario and his crew delivered the blow. Yazz and I just watched as they each pleaded for their lives. One chick even pleaded to suck my dick if I would spare her life. I could tell that she was a keeper back in the day. She had a very cute face, and her body wasn't bad. But somewhere between today and yesterday, the streets got a hold of her. What once was pretty became dirty and worn out. Yazz punched the shit out of her as she approached me. Yazz caught her with the heel of her stiletto as she fell to the floor. Yazz pressed her heel into the hypes neck until she coughed uncontrollably. The chick lay there helpless and defenseless against Yazz.

Yazz didn't say a thing. She just stared at the useless life and the control she had over it. I pulled Yazz out of the scene, so Mario and his crew could finish up. I wanted to know the standard, who why and what. Who sent them?, Why they did it? And what else they knew? Mario was proficient in getting answers. And his crew knew how to clean up, so no messes were left behind. I would say we taught him well. I knew once he finished handling his business he would get at me. There was no need for us to stand there and watch. Besides I had already created a monster, there was no need to add fuel to that flame.

# "Letter To The Firm"

**Foxy Brown**

**Yazz**

Jay and I left the spot. I had told Jay before we left out I wanted to go out tonight, but first wanted some pizza. So we were head in this direct anyway. Handling business was just a detour to our plans for the evening. We rode back towards LA Nova's. I had placed the order ahead of time. By the time we got there our order was ready. There was nothing better than Buffalo Pizza. It was the one thing I missed most when we were away. I can't tell you how many times I wanted to have Jay call someone and have them pick some up and drive that shit all the way to Michigan for me. I knew if I asked he would find a way to make it happen. All the shit we have been through I knew he would take a bullet for me. So pizza was a small ask in the grand scheme of things.

Jay stood there looking at me as we parked the car and went inside to pick up our order.

"What you lookin' at?" I asked with sass.

"You Ma, You.." Jay replied

"You act like you like what you see" I sassed back

"Most def, Ma. I Like the way that dresses hug them curves and those legs look in them heels" Jay commented.

I blushed as the guy at the counter yelled: "Go get a room you two."

We both laughed.

Joey was cool. We looked out for him and his family's business. No one ever rolled up on their spot actin' a fool. Everyone knew they were protected. Anika went to school with members of their family, which made them family. And if there is anything I've learned is that this family looks after its own.

"Yo Ma, seriously, you all right?" Jay questioned.

"I'm good Papi" I replied.

"You was about to get dirty back there, don't think I didn't catch that" Jay continued.

I just smiled. I found it best not to reply. He was right; I was ready to get dirty. That nasty bitch had it coming to her. Not because she propositioned Jay, but for being in that situation. How you gonna be a mother and a crackhead. A nasty one at that. I know, judgmental right? But I just can't make excuses for women who choose that life. Jay knew how I felt, but my hatred for those type of women grew even more as I became engulfed in this life with the FAM.

"Come here Yazz" Jay motioned as he grabbed my hand.

I walked into his open legs as he was posted up on his car. He kissed me gently and placed his hand on my ass. It was like the old days. Me and my girls leaving the club and running into Jay and Que afterward. It was a familiar touch. It was a memory and a feeling I longed for more often. I knew as long as he held me and loved me the way he did I was safe. But I also knew being in this life meant one day leaving that safe zone and getting dirty. Either way, I was prepared. And Jay knew it.

# "Can't Knock the Hustle"

-Jay Z

**Que**

"I can't even have a moment to take care of Ma and my seed without some shit poppin' off. Please explain to me how some crackheads stroll up in my shit and take from me? Because that's the shit, you tryna shove down my throat. You expect me to eat that shit and be ok? Is that what you are telling me, Mario? It that what I'm hearing Jay?" I spoke sternly looking at both these niggas in the face.

"Que, we took care of it. They were harmless, no real intel, nothing to report." Mario stated looking me in the eyes

"Mario's right Que. They were sloppy; it was basic shit. Hypes just tryna get high. If I thought it was anything else, you know I would have told you sooner. Hell, the whole city would be on lock right now. They were basic and simple, and Mario took care of it" Jay chimed in.

"Yo son, if they were so basic, then how the fuck they roll up in there and take shit? Doesn't do that kid. Basic niggas will beg for a crumb, try to sell you some broken shit, but never in the 20 years of sitting from this seat, has basic ever come up against the FAM. So now that I sit in the top seat, yall expect me to be ok with basic ass niggas, hypes at that, taking from the FAM. ME!" I yelled with authority.

"Yall need to get yall dicks out yo pussies and think about this shit, cause this shit don't even make sense." I flexed as I pushed away from the table and sipped on the cup of orange juice the waitress just brought over to me.

The table was quiet as hell. I knew then that dem niggas were slippin'. Everyone happy to be back in the Buffalo, they think shit is back to normal. But ain't nuttin' normal about this scenario.

"Yo, listen, I know we happy to be back, and everything seems like is all good. All I'm saying is this shit don't feel right to me. So before I let yall dismiss this, make sure ain't no other shit going on. We have been here before, and before it happens on my watch, make sure our shit is tight. Tighter than tight, you feel me?" I said in a no-nonsense tone.

"Jay, I need you to go to NYC to meet with the connect. Make sure our relationship is straight and find out what The Brothers hear from the streets. Mario, you need to visit the territories. Start in Michigan, head over to Chicago. I want a report from every state we in. After you're done with the Midwest, head south down to the Carolinas and swing back north, report back to me daily. Let me know what you hear and see. It's time for a road trip fellas. Ain't no time for site sightseeing; you need to make sure the territory is secure. Yall need to make sure that everyone under your watch is on the up and up. Know your peeps, listen, and most importantly watch. Everything you hear don't always match up to what you see. If everything is copacetic, then good, but if my gut is right, yall better be the first to squash this shit, before anything else pop off."

They agreed. We finished our breakfast at the cafe located on the first floor of the hotel Anika, and I was staying at. We went over the month's numbers, and I gave direction for deposits that needed to be made. I had faith in my niggas to handle business while I took care of Anika and my seed. Plus Uncle Clio had their backs. Hopefully, if all went well, Anika would be able to travel by the end of the week, and I could get her home. I told them both to remember what I said, "Ain't no house tighter than ours. So make sure I'm not a liar" I spoke as they both got up to exit the Cafe.

"Jay let me holla at you. Mario waits in the car." I spoke up

"Jay, how the hell did you not catch this shit? Mario takes your lead, so if you cosign this bullshit, he on board. You should have caught this. What's going on? Is there something you need to tell me?" I questioned.

"Que, you right, I should have caught this. I didn't. It won't happen again. I've been distracted worrying about Yazz." Jay answered.

"Yazz, what the fucks going on with her? I asked

"Que, that shit that happened in Detroit fucked her up. That innocent Yazz we knew is gone. She on a whole new level. Sometimes I feel like she gone do some damage in a bad way." Jay explained.

"That's fucked up Jay that shit would fuck anyone up. She gone be ok, right? Is there anything I can do to help?" I asked.

"Yeah, she was gone be ok. We gone be ok. It's just this shit is blowing my mind" Jay sounded off.

"Tighten it up then Nigga. Handle your business, but remember the FAM comes first" I replied.

"Done" Jay confirmed.

We dapped, and Jay exited the cafe. I watched as the town car that Jay and Mario arrived in drove away.

Waiting for the elevator, I could not help but think about the break-in. How is it that the tightest house in the City, let alone State was able to be penetrated? Everyone feared the wrath of the FAM, and my rep was no different. Niggas, bitches, whites, Latinos, arbics all knew who the fuck I was and who I represented. And no one knew this better than a crackhead. Hypes were clever, but not that damn good. The security in our drop and dope houses was top notch, and I upgraded things once I was named the head of the family just in case someone wanted to make a move. Now you are telling me some crackheads succeeded. I just can't and won't believe that shit.

But, I know one thing, I won't rest until I find out what's going on. I haven't survived in this game this long not to check everything. I thought as I rode the elevator up to the top floor. As the doors opened and I heard the ding from the elevator announcing my arrival to the penthouse, it occurred to me - Inside Job. First thought is the right thought and the only. Someone was on the hunt and tryna make a move. But I was ready for the kill. Defending the FAM was my life, and no one was ever gonna fuck up business or the cash flow on my watch. My gut was never wrong, and it was telling me we had beef, and it wasn't from strangers, it was internal.

# "Still in Love"

### - Brian McKnight

## Anika

Waking up with Que here has been a dream I've had since the day he left. He's been so attentive, so caring, and most important so apologetic. I told him that I understood. I may not agree with what happened, but that's the life he leads. We've had a chance to talk over the last couple of days. I do mean talk. I was calm enough to put my emotions aside so that he and I could put everything on the table. I told him about my engagement to Aaron. That when he left Aaron took care of me, loved me, and made me feel safe. That outside of him, I had not known another person I felt I could give my heart too. Que asked if I loved Aaron. I could see in his eyes the hurt this conversation was causing him. It was almost a mirror image of the pain I felt when he left me. I grieved for his pain and the hurt his heart was feeling. But I had to be honest. I told Que that I did love Aaron. That he was there for me when I needed someone. He was kind and gentle. I told him that after the baby was born, we had plans to get married. That the wedding was less than two months away.

But the truth was, I have only been in love with Que. My heart could not belong to anyone other than Que. While I knew I could grow to love Aaron, being in love was something I knew I would never have to try to be in with Que, I was already there. Yeah, I was mad at him, but underneath it all, I would always be in love with him. It was why the last eight months of my life felt incomplete because I'd always imagined it with Que. What I did not tell him was that the baby was his. He may know in his heart, but I was not ready to give him this power over me. I knew eventually I would need to tell him, but I also knew I would need to tell Aaron. I had lead him to believe that the baby was his. I never said it was, he just assumed, and I never said no it wasn't, which makes me all the more horrible. Breaking Aaron's heart was not something that I had ever intended to do, but I knew soon enough this day would come. Either Que would come back and demand answers, or I would have to explain to Aaron why our baby resembles another man.

Que tried to be as understanding as he could be. There were many empty sighs during our conversations. He knew me, and he knew that he broke my heart and that I would eventually move on from our relationship. I just don't think he thought it would happen so fast. But, I knew that Que would never give up, I could see it in his eyes. I knew that Que would stop at nothing to right his wrong. He would make this up to me one way and some day. For now, I just enjoyed our private welcome home celebration, even if it was no more than me sitting in the bed and him holding me. I knew that I was going to have to make some decisions and soon. Either way, It was about me and the baby. I just hope love could last through everything that was about to come next.

# "All That I Got is You"

**- Ghostface Killah**

**Que**

Spending time focused on work gave me a break I needed from the harsh reality of Anika and I. Damn, Shorty told me that she loved that nigga. I didn't think about all the pain I had caused let alone that pain pushing her into another niggas arms. It was way too much for me. I almost teared up and broke down and cried as I listened to her tell me about their plans. Plans that were supposed to be with me. Hell, Anika was always the woman I wanted to call wife. The truth was it killed me to think about another man, Aaron touching and loving her. I think about these past eight months and how every day they grew closer.

The anger inside me grew just thinking about it, but I had to understand or at least give Anika a chance to figure out what she wanted. After all, she was carrying my baby. We would always have that connection. BULLSHIT!! Fuck that sentimental shit, Anika was mine!! And I'll play this game until I've had enough. I'd show up at the wedding and take her then if I needed too. Hell, I'll take her now; remind her that I don't lose and that I get what I want. And right now I want her. Ain't no nigga got her heart like I do. And this time, I'll never take it for granted.

I walked back into the penthouse. The maids were fast at work cleaning and dusting. Anika was just getting out of bed. She was getting ready to take a shower. I watched her from the bedroom door. She undressed as I admired her accentuated curves. She was the most beautiful woman that I have ever seen. Her skin glowed like a tanning beach in the summertime. And that belly! How I loved the way, she did pregnancy. Her breast was erect, perky and swollen. They were the perfect handful of pleasure. I looked on in awe as she turned to catch me admiring her from a distance. She smiled and shyly walked into the bathroom au suite, I followed. Entranced by the way she moved, I watched as she began to touch her body. She was still my angel, angelic and sweet.

The lather from the loafer ball glistens as it covered her body. Mesmerized, I grabbed the loofah ball and insisted on helping. I climbed into the shower clothes and all. I touched her lower leg. I was lathering up her calves, knees, and thighs. Everywhere the loofah touched I kissed. Allowing Anika to balance her curvy body, I placed her foot on my bended knee, and I washed her feet, kissing all ten toes. I heard her moan as I sucked and kissed my way past her butt cheeks and up her back, washing and kissing my way to her neck and shoulders. There I was soaking wet in my designer clothing, Bally leather shoes, and my Rolex, not giving a damn about anything except getting my girl back. I kissed her from front to back; drank beads of water off her nipples and hips; I watched her watch me. Our eyes locked as she watched me lick and suck her inner thighs. She held onto me as I balanced her in my hands. She moaned. Her tears blended into the streams of water that covered her body. She held onto me as I took what was long overdue.

Once I was done, and her body stopped convulsing and shaking with ecstasy, I picked her up and carried her into the bedroom. I placed her on the bed as I removed my shirt and shoes. She unbuckled my belt, and unzipped my jeans; they fell to the floor. She kissed me, and I gave her my tongue. She sucked the sweetness of her juice off of my lips and tongue. It made my manhood hard as hell. I missed feeling like this, feeling complete satisfaction, being next to her like this. She sat there on the edge of the bed taking my fully erected penis into her mouth. She controlled me as my eyes rolled back in my head and my knees gave way to her long strokes and gentle touch. She sucked me like she missed me. Like I was her favorite lollipop, and there was a surprise hidden inside. She stroked me and stroked me, making exotic sounds as she went up and down my rock hard shaft. My body shook, and my knees grew weak. I was home. I was where I needed to be.

At this moment the way she took me was nothing short of love; real Love, the feeling I got only from Anika's touch. She stroked and stroked, making the shaft of my dick wetter and harder. With her hands, she massaged her saliva into my balls and up and down my pipe as she sucked the head and teased me by slapping her tongue on the tip. She went up and down taking me all the way in touching her tonsils and opening her airway. I felt the warmth of her inside begging me to explode. She handled me and tortured me and forced me to let go and explode. I cried out in anger, pain, joy, and peace as she drank eight months of sorrow away, as she took my seed and welcomed us home.

# "Touch Me Tease Me"

**- Case ft. Foxy Brown**

**Anika**

I wanted him. I needed him. I had waited for this moment for so long.

"It's ok. I promise you; the baby will be ok" I stated as I sensed his hesitance.

"Are you sure?" Que asked.

"I did not answer, but instead I pulled him down on me and took the still erect dick and placed it into my wet Orpheus. It was just as I remembered, long, thick, and hard. His strokes instantly awakened my senses and our baby. As Que drummed his way into me, our baby moved and played along. It freaked Que out. I could tell he thought he was hurting the baby. I whispered, "don't stop" and he obliged. I watched him as he rode me with such gentleness and care. I could feel my body exploding with joy all over his dick with each stroke. I could feel my lips wrapping themselves around that massive dick and welcoming it home the way my mouth welcomed him just minutes before.

"Your home baby, welcome home" I whispered as his dick went deeper and deeper with each stroke. I moaned and hissed as he cupped my breast and sucked my strawberry shaped nipples. I tingled with pleasure and craved more and more. I maneuvered my way on top of him and with caution began to ride his dick. The stimulation was awesome. My pussy was so wet from squirting on his dick that it made him harder and hungrier from the excitement. I rode him caressing the dick as I went up and down and back and forth while sitting on his lap. He held me tight as I bounced on him and the baby moved as mommy and daddy played. He kissed me; I kissed him. I rode him until I was out of gas and could not take the pleasure his dick bestowed onto me.

## Que

I turned her sweaty body over as she positioned herself on all fours. I entered her from behind as she screamed in the most beautiful whispers of satisfaction. I held onto her now accentuated hips and pounded my dick into her. I fucked her almost like I was beating her for allowing another nigga to have what is mine. I punished her and myself for the eight months of absenteeism. I entered her for the pain and the joy of our past and our future. I gave her all my tears with each stroke. Every time she bucked back, I administered discipline. I slapped Anika's ass with the force of four Nuns at a Catholic school administering correction. The thought of another man enjoying her this way caused my anger to grow and my passion for deepening. She was mine, body, and soul. And with all that I had, I planted my seed deep into her as we both came to the sounds of our beating hearts.

I held her in my arms. I could feel the baby moving. I watched as he moved and made imprints of himself into Anika's belly. We played follow daddy's hand and kick the belly. Anika laughed and smiled as I spoke to our unborn child. It was the connection I waited eight months for and solidified in my heart that the child was mine. It was beautiful.  I promised my son that I would always be there for him, that I love his mother more than I loved myself, and that I would never allow anyone or thing to hurt either of them. I rested my head on her belly and listened to the absurd sounds my son made as Anika rubbed my head. Eight months of missing out on this, not being here, I will never forgive myself. But know, right here, this felt right, it felt pure. I wanted this moment always, and I would stop at nothing to get it. Anika was mine, and I was hers. It was time to set the record straight.

# "Watch Dem Niggas"

**- Nas**

## Mario

The more I thought about what Que said, the more I thought he was right. Not that crack heads aren't crafty and sly, but going up against the FAM was like tryna break into Fort Knox. We were impregnable. No way, no how, so something else is going on. This put me on high alert. Now I can see why Que questioned us like that. Well, I won't get caught sleepin' again, we should have caught this one. Live and learn; I thought to myself as Big L drove us down the I-75. We were leaving Kentucky headed down to Alabama and over to Georgia then up the eastern coast. Thanks to Que, the FAM's territory expanded to include most of the Midwest states. When Que was sent to Michigan, He and Jay set out to take on

Wisconsin, Minnesota, Iowa, Missouri on down to Arkansas. They damn near captured the country and divided it into two. It was now us against everyone else. Nothing happens in our territory without Que's approval or knowing about it. And with such a large area to cover it was important that he had the right niggas in place.

I had reported back to Que daily. With every stop, we were greeted like kings. They laid out bitches and drinks for us to indulge in. But before there could be any celebrations, I had to handle business. I looked over each station's books and men. Asked the necessary questions to make sure they knew the law and followed protocol. No stone left unturned or unseen, plus it was a loyalty check. Que placed these niggas in the respective places because he knew they would be loyal to the FAM and him, which now meant they were loyal to me. So far everything was all good. Not only are those niggas loyal but their shit was just as tight as the operation in Buffalo. Many of them were still talking about Que's inaugural ceremony. How lit that shit was and all the lavish gifts he gave those under him. I guess they tried to mimic that shit, because they showed out for your boy, had a nigga feeling real nice. I kept it straight, no drugs, a few drinks to show respect, but the honey... that was always a distraction.

We made our way to South Carolina. After a week on the road meeting family and new faces, it was good to be around cousins, aunts, and uncles that I grew up with. Al B. pulled up to my Auntie Rose's house; we were staying with her. She was my grandmother's sister. There was no one like my Auntie Rose. As a kid, she would spoil the hell out of me. It made my siblings mad that I was her favorite, and, her homemade biscuits made a nigga wanna dance. She would make them shits and serve them hot right out the oven with some syrup and butter. Al B pulled into the driveway and opened my door. I walked up to the front porch to be greeted by my aunt and her daughter, Pam. There were hugs and kisses, and even cheek pinching. It was one of the few times that I allowed myself to be soft. She welcomed me into her home and showed us all where we would be sleeping. Auntie Rose had a modest, but large home. Her intake from the business had done her well. She never flaunted her wealth like most in the family. Her car was a modest older model Cadillac. She even still drove her late husband's F150 that was at least 20 years old. She lived on a farm just outside of Calhoun Falls which is just west of Greenville. And as promised, Aunt Rose had laid out a welcome brunch suitable for a king or president. We all sat down and enjoyed ourselves. It wasn't long before Auntie Rose spilled the beans.

Auntie Rose started droppin' hints that shit ain't right in South Carolina.

"They mad at the board" she would say as she took a fork full of field peas. "Yup they are talking foolishly" she continued. "All I know is that they better not mess up my cut. I will fuck a country nigga ass up if they mess up my money" she laughed as my cousin Pam looked on mortified.

"What Ma is tryna say is.." Pam started but was interrupted by Auntie Rose.

"I ain't tryna say shit, but the truth and shame the devil." She added.

"I'm happy you here Mario. We need you and your cousins from up north. Yall can straighten some shit out down here. I don't know if the four of yall gone be enough, but it's a start."

I just smiled and nodded and took mental notes of everything she said. There was one thing I knew for sure; Auntie Rose wasn't any liar. She may have been old, but she knew what she was talking about. When it came to her money, Auntie Rose's 87-year-old mind was a sharp as a machete. There was some truth in the hints she was dropping, and I was catching every last crumb.

The next morning, I rose early to the sweet smell of bacon and biscuits. Aunt Rose was at it again. We drank and laughed all night long, and now she was up early this morning making breakfast. I went down to greet her with a kiss. It was just her and I in the kitchen. She spoke candidly and stern.

"Mario, I know I drank last night, but everything I said was the truth. You need to tell Que we gotta problem down here."

"Auntie Rose don't you worry about nothing. That's why I'm here. If something ain't right

I'll know, and we will act accordingly." I assured her.

"Babe, now listen. Ain't no need to figure shit out. They mad at the north. Talkin' bout, we got overlooked, overlooked my ass. These country ass niggas can't get right to save themselves let alone run the family business. You be careful Mario, 'cause I swear something happens to my favorite nephew, I'm coming out of retirement and Imma kill every got damn body." she laughed.

"Won't be no need for that Auntie" I laughed with her.

"But seriously Mario, them niggas are plottin' something. Last few family gatherings there were secret meetings, and when I said something about it, they damn near gave me the look of death. I don't trust 'em. Shit, they can't even come over here no more. They up to something and it ain't good. You go into Columbia be ready to fight, 'cause them niggas ain't gone be happy to see you. Don't expect any warm greeting, and watch them eyes. Niggas gonna be lying, puttin' on acts, all awhile plottin'. It doesn't feel good. My bones tellin' me something bad is going down." she spoke.

"Auntie Rose you said that they mad at the north, why they mad?" I asked.

"They mad that Que sittin' in that chair; mad that a whole generation been overlooked. I would say that's what's causing this uproar. They didn't say it, but I know baby." she insisted.

"Auntie, why do you think Que was placed at the head of the family?" I asked.

"Baby, your father, and Pam's generation were proud people. They had a new found freedom. They wanted so desperately to be a part of the white man's world that the smart ones went and got educated. Gone off to dem colleges and universities. No one with any sense was left to work for the family. They looked down on the money we made, said it was dirty. Well, that left the scraps at the bottom of the barrel to inherit the kingdom. When I sat on the board, we made a promise that no one from that generation would sit at the head of this family. Now that did not mean just the north or south; it meant both. They took for granted who we were and the legacy of the family. Oh, it was good for buyin' dem houses, and dem fancy cars, and that education n' shit. But we chose a long time ago that as punishment for their arrogance, they would be overlooked. So you see baby, it defaulted to the next generation after that, the grandbabies. We made sure that each family member was well represented for consideration. We sent the best of each house to be groomed every summer in Buffalo. They played and got a chance to know each other, but they were also introduced to the family business. It was time to see who rose to the top. Que was always at the top. Till this day Que was always at the top. He expanded the business, he takes care of business, and most important, he respects the game. That was key. He respects the game and those who came before him, the board and the operations. We knew it would be Que, just like I knew you would be where you are. Don't you think we groomed you too? So open your eyes baby; listen. If I say it ain't right, it ain't right down here, and it's gonna take more than the four of yall to come down here and fix what's wrong. So make that call and then go into Columbia. Your family down here ain't loyal to the FAM. Which means they ain't loyal to you or Que" she stated kissing me on the cheek.

I felt the warning; Auntie Rose had painted a clear enough picture for me. I called Que and told him what Auntie Rose said. Que gave direction. He was sending some help my way, and I called in soldiers from other territories. We had sixteen hours before I was going to be heading into Columbia. I wasn't sure how widespread this fuckery had reached, so I had soldiers heading to North Carolina. These sets of family members seemed to be the closest. I knew if one jumped then they both would jump. The rest of this shit I would need to see on my own. Either way, the cancer was about to be flushed out. It did not matter blood or water if you stand against the FAM it was just a matter of time before you fall. South Carolina was about to feel the wrath of the FAM, and my gut is telling me the drought was over. It was about to rain blood, and I was going to be knee deep in it.

# "Formula"

**- The D.O.C**

**Jay**

I arrived in NYC at 11:50. My plane landed at LaGuardia Airport. I claimed my luggage and headed to the front door. There was a white man holding up a sign with my name on it. I approached his surprise, and he quickly took my bags, placed them in the trunk of his black town car, and off we drove. I was staying at the Hilton Midtown Manhattan. It was right off of 6th ave; I had stayed there plenty of times in the past. It was a good midpoint for any meetings that I need to attend. I could quickly make my way around town and still be able to hop on the subway to get to Queens or the Boogie Down if I had too. Either way, it kept me away from the riff-raff and yet wasn't too stuffy of an atmosphere that I could not relax. We pulled up to the Hotel in what seemed like an eternity of driving. The traffic here was always on horrible. There was always a traffic jam to catch or an accident to see. New Yorkers were too damn aggressive when it came to driving, and that applied not only to the city but the whole damn state. The driver got my luggage out the car, and I entered the lobby of the hotel. Stacey, a petite white young lady, was there to greet me. After a few minutes of small talk, I was registered and had received the key to my room.

I had taken a short nap. It was rare that I had a chance to rest, let alone sleep, so I took advantage of the situation. I took a shower and got dressed for my first meeting. I took a cab to a club The Brothers wanted to meet at. Now, The Brothers were different. The FAM had been dealing with their family for decades. Que and I were used to dealing with their father, until his untimely death. That is when his sons took over for their family. Que and I showed our respect for their newly assigned delegation by attending their family function to honor their father, and celebrate the passing of the torch. And boy could they party. There was drinks following and every drug known to mankind being passed out, gift wrapped like it was candy. Que and I sat back and watched as we saw how the others lived. But yeah these boys were different, they marched to a beat all their own. And who the fucks gonna say something? Not I. With all that money and power you can be as crazy and eccentric as you want. The last thing you want to do is make someone with that kind of connection and that much money mad or upset. Yo ass goes missing or turns up dead. Besides, in our business, you learn that it's all about the money. Who cares what or who you fuck, what you look like, or any other fucked up fetishes you have. The only thing that matters is the paper.

We pulled up to the club. I was early which was always good. I was dressed in a black custom made suit with a black shirt. I had on my Rolex; the one Que gave me as a gift and a pair of Black matted squared toe Stacy Adams shoes. I was sharp, and I was ready to do business. I walked into the club with the confidence of player. I had been here before, just never on my own, so this was new to me. In my new role, I would be conducting business like this all the time. I had learned over the years that you couldn't be nervous sitting at the table of trigga happy niggas. I gave my name to the hostess and was seated at a secluded table in the back of the club. It was dimly lit, but I was seated perfectly to be able to view everyone's coming and goings in the club. As a mental note to self, I never sat with my back to the door. It was an easy way to get caught off guard. Before I could even sit down good. I heard the obnoxious antics of The Brothers coming from across the club. I could hear them before I could see them. They were being escorted over to the table. I stood to shake their hands and was quickly grabbed into a three-way hug fest.

We ordered drinks and quickly caught up on each other families. I had learned from Que and those before us that when visiting partners was always customary to bring gifts. It was a token of appreciation for the business relationship. The Brothers were Italians; their family was immigrants from Sicily. Although they were Sicilians, it was rare that their mother had an opportunity to visit her family back home. So we knew she treasured authentic items for the island. I had ordered two cases of rare Marsala Vino from a wine dealer connect I know. Each bottle is valued over $1000.00, so a single case will run you $24k. I was giving them two cases. I waved to have the waitress bring over the cases of wine to the table to present to my guest. They were ecstatic when I presented the gift.

"A gift from Que and the Fam." I gestured.

They immediately opened the bottle, then sniffed, rolled and savored the aroma of the wine. They took a swig and allowed the flavors to resonate on their tongues, before spitting it out into a bucket. I took the smiles on their faces as a sign that I had done good.

"Salute," The twins said as the wine glasses made the standard clink sound.

"Thank you, Thank you," they spoke in unison.

"I thought that you both should know how appreciative the FAM is of our continued partnership. I'd like to toast to many more years of success and growth for both of our families."

"Salute"

"Salute" They spoke as the clinking of glasses.

"Jay, nothing would please us more. Our families have known each other for decades. Hell, we played together at some of the meetings our fathers and grandfathers had. Your family has been the main source of business for us in the country. We are exclusively devoted to you" spoke one twin.

"Yes Jay, the money we make together keeps both of our houses healthy. It is with this reason that we agreed to this meeting" spoke the other twin.

The tone of the conversation turned serious. I could feel there was something weighing heavy on their minds.

"Brothers, there has never been any secrets kept between our families. Let's not start now. If there is something, I should know, Please speak freely" I insisted.

"Jay there is turmoil in your house" spoke one brother

"Yass Jay, this cannot be good for business." spoke the other.

"We see a disruption in the flow of money, this we cannot have" spoke the first twin.

"Wait for what…? Slow down. What the fuck are you talking about?" I questioned.

"Jay, you don't know? You don't know?" They chatted between themselves.

"Naw I don't know. What the fuck are yall talking about." I asked again annoyed.

"Jay, we were contacted by a representative of your family who wants to do business directly with us. We were told that they were branched off from the FAM and needed a supplier. Jay, they wanted to arrange a meeting." They spoke in unison.

"WHAT?!" I replied.

"Yass Jay. His names was umm. Umm, Cornelius. Yeah, his name was Cornelius. He said he was a representative of your family from South Carolina." one twin spoke.

"We did not want to cause any beef. This is not how we do business. We cannot be a supplier to both. We told them, no, but that won't stop them from going elsewhere."

"Yeah Jay, you have a problem. We suggest you clean it up before we have to find a new buyer." spoke the other twin.

"There will be no need for that. I'll take care of this issue. Nothing will interfere with our money arrangements." I started making myself very clear.

"We hope so Jay. It would be a shame if after all these years we have to go somewhere else. We like you and Que, but this is business, you understand" one twin spoke up.

"Yeah, I understand. Gentlemen, if you'll excuse me, I need to end our meeting. Please stay and enjoy yourselves, It is on me" I spoke as I stood to shake their hands and made my way to the front door. I had made the waitress aware to keep the liquor flowing for them and to send over a few hot guys and girls for them to have fun with. I never knew what they preferred, it all depended on their mood and day of the week. My driver had pulled the car up to the front door, I hopped in and headed back to the hotel.

"DAMNIT!" I yelled. Que is not gonna like this shit!

# "O.P.P"

**- Naughty By Nature**

**Aaron**

Damn! I haven't heard from Anika in weeks. Every time I call she's never home, and now the answering machine is full. I'm sure everything is ok. I just want to hear my baby girl's voice. Maybe this weekend I would fly back to Buffalo and check in on her. I tried calling one last time before I headed out to the club. No answer. Oh well. I tried. I'm sure mommy is out hanging with her girls, and I am about to do the same. We had ridden down to Miami after practice today. It was me and few of my teammates. I had rented a candy apple red Lamborghini for the weekend. It was bad ass. It was a pussy magnet, and if there was one thing I knew about this weekend, my dick was getting into some new pussy. Miami pussy.

I pulled up to the hottest nightclub in the city. The valet opened the door, and I stepped out in style. There was a line of wannabes standing outside; all tryna get into the club. I walked straight to the front of the line and greeted the bouncer; I was let right in. The DJ was jammin'. It was packed with niggas, ballers and bitches galore. I got an instant hard-on just thinking about the prospects I was going to walk away with tonight. I was escorted to VIP and a table that had been reserved for me and my boys. A few of my teammates were already in here. I could see CJ dancing with some honey. Mike and Roger were toasting it up with a few shorties of their own. I was late to the party.

"WHAT'S UP!" I yelled as I sat down.

"What's up player," Mike said leaning in to give me dap.

"Shit homie, we thought you wasn't coming, thought maybe ya girl had that baby or something" Roger added as we exchanged greetings.

"Naw bro, she still holding on to that baby. I just couldn't get a hold of her again." I replied.

"Man she ok. She would call if she needed something" Mike suggested.

"True dat nigga" Roger chimed in.

"I know. Yall right." I agreed. "Yo, what I got to do to get a few bottles poppin' over here?" I finished waving for the server to come over to the table. "Shiiid, until I say I do, I'm single, and right now I need honey that's ready to party" I stated searching the club for my next victim.

I made my way down to the dance floor. There was this Latina shorty who had been eyin' me. She would dance and look my way every once in a while. She flung her hair in that naughty girl way beckoning me to pull it. She was wearing a white mini dress. It was so damn short it barely covers her ass. She had legs and curves, with the most beautiful olive complexion this side of the equator. I made my way over to her as she was spinning around. She noticed that I was there and smiled. I placed my hand on her waist and pulled her into me. She began to slow whine on me. I know she could feel the hard rock that was being held back in my pants. We danced, and I held onto her like she belonged to me. I kissed her neck and felt her up. I even grabbed her ass and cuffed it pushing her further and further into me. She smelled good, and the heat we were creating on the dance floor made me want her even more. I danced with her and her friends. And for the rest of the night, she was mine.

I took her up to VIP. We had drinks and talked. She sat on my lap as I whispered in her ear. My hands were all over her, and she was a willing participant. Before I knew it, she had her hands down my pants caressing my manhood. Ma knew what she was doing. I just sat back and allowed her to enjoy what I would soon give to her. With each stroke, my dick would get swollen. I was ready to bust through my cream colored linen pants. Without saying a word, she removed her hand from my pants, grabbed my hand and lead me to the bathroom in the VIP area. We entered the women's bathroom. There were a few ladies in there. They all looked stunned to see me following behind her. But not stunned enough to scream, which told me that they had seen this type of behavior before, and was aware of what was happening next. She took me into the stall and began to unzip my pants. She took hold of my dick and placed it in her mouth. Her pretty pink lips wrapped around my penis like she was sucking on a popsicle. Ma knew how to work it too. I stood there as she sucked and slurped me down. I looked down at her as she enjoyed my growing manhood beating her tonsils. I grabbed her hair and held on to her, guiding her head back and forth at a pace that mimicked a steady fuck.

I removed her dress. She wasn't wearing any panties. Her breast were full and perky. She was evenly proportioned with thighs to match. She pulled my pants down as I picked her up and placed her on my rock hard dick. I slid into her with force. She held on tight as she bounced her olive toned body on my dick. Up and down she went as I held her ass and she screamed in pleasure. She bounced and bounced like I was a carnival ride and she was a thrill seeker. I rammed my dick into her with every downward stroke she took. Her breast wiggled as I bounced her on me again and again. Up and down she went massaging my dick with her tight pussy. I could feel her climax as she exploded with juice. I took my dick out of her pussy and placed in at the entrance of her ass and without asking, forced my way into her. She screamed with excitement and pain. My massive cock tore her opening and made its way all the way inside her. I grabbed her ass cheeks and rammed her into my dick as she caught her breath and began to join in. I stood there in the bathroom stall, as she rode my dick with her ass, channeling her riding skills just as she had done a few minutes earlier. I fucked her good, and her tight ass was mine. I fucked her and fucked her until I came. I took her off of me and grabbed some tissue and cleaned myself off. She was putting her dress back on, and I could see my seamen dripping down the back of her legs. I squirted a nice load into her ass. I laughed as I thought about that. She cleaned herself off, and when she was done, we opened the door to the stall. We were met with applause as a group of ladies were in the bathroom admiring our performance. As we were walking out, a young black hottie grabbed my hand.

"Can I go for a ride too?" she asked.

Not one to turn down in need. I smiled at the Latino ma, said goodbye, and allowed the big booty honey to take the lead. She took me into the same bathroom stall I had just exited. It was time for round two and looking at this chocolate honey; I could tell she was a freak. My dick was getting hard just thinking about the tricks she was about to do. Down she went to greet my manhood, and all I could think about was if Anika ever found out., I'd lose everything. But this honey had tricks, and her tongue was already doing things to me. I'll have to think about…. yeah…about…that…shit…later.

# "Shame on a Nigga"

**- Wu-Tang Clan**

**Que**

So we have a problem. South Carolina. Niggas by blood tryna play me softly. Niggas I've been taken care of damn near my whole life, tryna run game on a nigga strong. Ok. Well, now they like any other nigga comin' at me. I thought to myself. Uncle Clio was sitting at the dining room table. He was calm, cool and collected. I could tell that he was in deep thought. He always took his time before he spoke. I took it as a sign of wisdom being spoken by a god. His years in the game deserved that much acknowledgment. Inside I was fuming. Buffalo had been penetrated by someone from the south working with these niggas. It might be an isolated individual, or it could be more. Either way, an example was going to be made. Uncle Clio sat there staring at me. I could tell he knew I grew angrier as the seconds passed.

"Que, what's our next step" Uncle Clio asked.

"My gut told me something was going down. Just never figured it to be family. Nonetheless, it had to be dealt with. We can't have members of the organization going rogue. It was bad for business and the FAM name." I stated.

"Your right. So what's the next move now that you know" Asked Uncle Clio.

"I already called a meeting with the board. It's set for tomorrow Morning at 10 am. I'm flying everyone in. I have cars picking everyone up from the airport. We are meeting here. I know that this space is safe. The staff will be dismissed for the morning. We will have freedom to speak candidly. In the meantime, Mario and a few crews are headed to Columbia, SC. I also sent a few cousins to stay with Auntie Rose until this shit blows over. Jay is also headed down to North Carolina. With the families down there being so close it was best we neutralize both of them at the same time. Jay and Mario will check in after the meeting tomorrow awaiting further instructions. And I have Yazz and Monica keeping watch for me on the crew that ran the house that was popped." I stated.

"Que, taking out family is different than going up against enemies. They know your weaknesses. More importantly, they know you. Better than anyone else, they know you, names and dates. Make sure if you go in it's to wipe out everyone. Under these circumstances, survivors become sworn enemies for life, and we can't have sons and daughters coming back on us. Just know that once you kill family there, is no going back. It's either them or us." Uncle Clio spoke clearly.

I nodded in agreement.

The alarm went off at 6 am. I woke up from what little sleep I received. My mind was heavy with the thought of warring with flesh and blood, and Anika and the baby. While I knew one would be ok, the thought of killing blood weighed heaviest. I can't believe these niggas. We talking about cousins I grew up with. People I hugged and kissed, loved, sat at the table with and broke bread. It got me to thinking about the night of my inauguration. At the party, dudes were coming and going. I sat there in VIP watching. Learning the faces and judging the looks on everyone's faces. There were a few niggas that caught my eye.

I had watched them. They smiled, but their eyes sounded off alarms.

At the time I could not tell if it was just niggas tryna front and be hard, or if it was the long trip up north, or any number of shitty reasons dudes look like they ready for war. Hell, in this game you can't afford to look weak. So the meaner the mug, the harder the rep. But it was something about these niggas. I just could not put my finger on it at the time. And because I was not entertaining anyone in VIP that wasn't supposed to be there, they never got close enough to me to find out. All I know is they were from the south. Betcha I find out now.

I ran the shower and tried to wash away my stress. I knew that airplanes would be landing soon, so I needed to get my shit together. I quickly got dressed, dismissed the staff for the morning and prepared for the meeting. Before the staff left, they had placed fresh flowers out and made sure the dining room was set for 14. There was a call from the front desk announcing that 3 of my guest had arrived. I waited by the elevator and when it opened greeted, my aunt and uncles. One by one they arrived. I had coffee and tea ready and fresh croissants and other pastries. Once everyone had arrived, we went into the dining room to begin.

They ate the breakfast I had prepared by house caterers as I spoke. I went over what I had learned. I went over a plan to neutralize the situation and even account for the number casualties. I waited for an objection, but none came. My Aunt Donetta spoke first.

"Que, we have been waiting for this moment. We knew at some point the south would show its hand. You see, South Carolina has been upset for a while about the decisions the board makes. They are unhappy with our choice in leadership and how the money is divided." she spoke breaking the silence.

"We knew we would have to take down that part of the family, so we are on board with whatever measures you take to handle this situation." my uncle Mac continued.

"We are aware this means war. We also know that our beloved family members pose a direct threat to all of us and the future of family business. It is either them or us" cousin Matt said.

I nodded my head in agreeance. I knew that it had come down to this. They took a vote and cast

a unanimous decision. War it was and the death
of the family.

# "Just One of those days"

**- Monica**

**Yazz**

I wasn't at all mad that Jay had to make the trip to NYC. Shit, it didn't even bother me that he didn't ask if I wanted to join him. I just needed time to breathe. It seems like Jay, and I had been glued to each other over the past few months. Every time I turned around, he was there. But lately, I just needed some space, and I'm sure he feels the same. Him being gone would give me time to relax and hang out with my girls. Jay had told me that Anika was with Que in Toronto. I'm sure they had a lot to talk about. Hell Anika was pregnant, and the word was it was Que's. But the way everybody been talkin' 'bout Anika and Aaron, it could go either way. I just pray my girl knows what she's doing. Either way, I got her back, which is why I'm going to get to the bottom of some shit that Monica put me on to. Monica had told me about Aaron and some noise she had been hearing about him. The last thing I would ever want is my girl to be out here being played, let alone marrying this asshole if he ain't worthy. Monica believes that nigga is up to no good and between her and me, we were gonna find out.

I told Monica I would come by and scoop her up around 3 pm. There was a party tonight in Cleveland that we wanted to get to. I knew I need to get to the mall and find something to wear, so I headed out early. It felt good to be back in familiar settings. I loved knowing the names of the store at the mall. I knew what to expect. I knew what stores had what I was looking for, and which ones had no flava. Even the store clerks knew me. They had come to know my likes and dislikes, and also proceeded with caution when selecting outfits for me to try on or view.

When I was in Detroit, it was just hood and ghetto all the time. It was like every chick was rockin' the same shit; there was no originality. I swear I bought so much flavor to that scene, bitches didn't know how to take me. And I was on Jay's arm. They were looking and hatin' on me all the time. But yo, my shit was tight. There were even times that I caught crew tryna look at me, but Jay shut that shit down quickly. All I could do was laugh. I finally made my way around the mall and found a few pieces to rock tonight to the skate party. I also did Monica a favor and picked her up some shit I knew she would like. It would be fowl of me to show up to the party looking fly and have Monica looking crazy. Yeah, that would never happen. The way that bitch have niggas buying her shit, she probably already got newness hanging up in her closet, I thought to myself laughing out loud.

I pulled up to Monica's house. As one could predict, Monica was outside mackin' on some poor prey. This dude didn't have a clue what Monica was about to do to and with him. This poor sap got a whiff of Monica's pheromones, and now he just can't let go.

"Girl c'mon, we ain't got no time to be recruiting!" I laughed out loud to Monica.

"Bitch, I always go time for dick" Monica yelled back to me laughing as she finished up her conversation and walked back to the house.

"Don't be hatin' on your girl" Monica nudged me as we made our way into her room and she began to open the bag of goodies I picked up from the mall.

"Chick you know we ain't got time for no niggas right now. I'm tryna get to this party tonight, and you know we have to drive 4 hours to get there. Besides, there will be all kinds of man candy for you to choose from in Cleveland" I said passing her the bags that had items for her to choose from.

"Damn bitch this is cute," Monica said holding up one of the outfits I purchased.

"I thought you would like that with your nasty ass" I joking comment.

"Girl ain't nothing wrong with lace and leather" she joked back.

We quickly got dressed. Both of us checking ourselves in the full-length mirror. Makeup was on point and hair was laid. It was time to hit the road and get ready to party.

We were headed out the door when my pager went off. I checked the number it was Jay. I noticed the code he put in; it was an emergency. I hesitated but I knew I had to call him back.

He filled me in. I couldn't even get a word in. I could hear the grit in his voice. His tone was serious, and his words were stern. And as always I had his back. I had the FAM's back, and it was time for business.

"Change of plans Monica," I spoke

"What no Party tonight," she said sarcastically.

"Nah, we goin' to party just not in Cleveland," I stated.

It was time to handle some business. Que had given the word, and I was ready for some action. There was nothing hotter than two chicks dressed to kill and to handle business. I was trigga happy, and Monica was just ready to ride along.

# "4,3,2,1"

## - LL Cool J ft. Red Man, Method Man, DMX, and Canibus

**Mario**

I had been in South Carolina long enough to see that things were different down here. I'm not talking about the slow ass country talk these muthafuckas spit; I'm talking about the way the FAM is represented here. The corners was heavy, but the crews were weak. They were flashy ass niggas, plus I could tell they were using their product which was never a good sign. It was like amateur night at the Apollo. These clowns were too busy skinnin' and grinin' to even notice me walking their streets.

I had crews spread throughout the city of Columbus and the countrysides of the state. In order for us to clean house, we first needed to figure out the basics. Spot all the players and make sure that when we attack we hit hard and fast taking out the heart of the beast. Columbus was the heart of the FAM in South Carolina. Plus it's were that Judas Cornelius was at. Yeah, Jay filled me in on his punk ass, and I was all too familiar with him. Cornelius was my first cousin. His father was my grandma and Auntie Rose's brother. He was the youngest of six kids, which meant he was my age give or take a couple of years. I remember playing with his punk ass growing up. He was a tattle tell and a crybaby. Every time something didn't go his way he'd stump his country ass into the house and lie his way out of trouble or lie his way to an ass whooping from his cousins for getting us in trouble. From the sounds of it, nothing's changed.

Now, one would think with the moves these bamas been tryna make they would have their shit tight down here. Either they don't think we know, that us niggas from the north ain't really about that life, or they ain't scared. Either way, they gone learn soon enough. I was receiving reports from my team on the street, and we were close to making our move. We heard that these country ass niggas was planning a cookout. I thought it best that we make our move then. This way we could kill multiple birds with one stone. It was set, in three days blood would be shed, and the FAM would be reborn in the south.

I just got a page from Jay; he had just arrived in North Carolina. He had a few crews from the Midwest with him. Niggas Que had appointed while conducting business in Michigan. These Niggas was gritty and hungry. They were loyal and like most of us, about them Benjamins. They were hard and ruthless. You know, they kind of niggas that just don't give a fuck, hide your bitch cause they'll fuck her while you watch at gunpoint kinda shit. Yeah, they were them kind of dudes, and I loved it. Grimy as hell and loyal to the FAM.

Jay was going to handle business there and had already been planning his attack. Auntie Rose gave us the name of 2 cousins who she trusted. Gino and Bark were good dudes. They were loyal to Que and always reported back to Auntie Rose when shit wasn't on the up and up. They went undercover and began reporting back to Jay. There was going to be a family meeting outside of Fayetteville at some hotel. All the major players from the state would be there. Our intel told us that North Carolina was split. About half the family did not want to break away from Que and the north. But by not speaking up and taking this to Que, they had silently chosen a side. And per Que, it didn't matter; if they are sitting at that table on Saturday, then death is what was coming as an act of defiance to family or foe.

# "Taken in Blood"

**- Nas**


## Jay


It was the night before we cleaned house down here. I Had gone over the plan in my head over and over again. Made sure my crew was ready. I had covered all my angles. In my short time here I had managed to learn this country ass city as if it was my hood. I had timed getaway routes just in case the heat came down on us. I had made payments to individuals that were looking for a quick come up as a thank you for turning a blind eye. I had made friends with a few Police Officers that were on the take. I had money, guns, clips and silencers, cars and a gang of killers. My gut told me that this would by no means be easy, but I'd be damn if they get the drop on me and my crew. So, being prepared was a must.  I sat there in my room chillin' as much as I could.

I was ready, so was my crew. It was now just a waiting game. Tell that to my trigger happy finger.  These crab ass niggas had no idea what their disloyalty was about to cost them. All I could say was blood might be thicker than water, but water doesn't stain the carpet when it's spilled. This war was going to serve as a stain for generations to come.  A reminder of what happens when you cross the FAM. Run niggas run, 'cause the FAM is coming for dem asses, I thought as I closed my eyes and zoned out listing to Raekwon's Heaven and Hell.

# "If I Should Die"

- Jay Z

**Que**

"Anika, baby I'll be back by 10 pm tonight" I kissed her and rubbed her belly. I could tell she didn't want me to go. I had promised that I would not lie to her ever again. So when she asked, against my better judgment I brought her up to speed with everything that was happening, the short cute version. There was no reason for her to be concerned, especially after the scare we just had with her. I needed mommy and the baby to be as healthy and as stress-free as possible, but daddy needed to go and handle business. I'd be back and on time. I left the penthouse and headed downstairs to the town car that was waiting for me. I carried only a duffle bag and my passport. This was a business meeting I would not miss.

As we drove toward the airport, I sat there thinking about the conversation I had yesterday. Before I could even make the call to uncle Clio and the board, the phone in the penthouse rang. It was auntie Donnetta. She was sitting across the street in the little Cafe and wanted to speak in private. I told Anika I was running out for some fresh Croissants. She had come to love the ones with cream cheese baked in them; luckily we were out. I went across the street and was greeted by auntie Donnetta. She arrived in Toronto just about 30 minutes beforehand. I could tell from the look on her face whatever she had to say was serious.

"What brings you all this way, Auntie?" I asked kissing her on the cheek and sitting down at the table she made home.

"Que, e'ry since you were a child I could tell when you were up to something. I knew when things didn't sit well with you, that you would defend, even takeover a situation, make sure that things went just so. And nothing's changed. Baby, we the board want you to sit this fight out. You need to let Jay and Mario handle this. It is too much of a risk for you and the FAM." she spoke with authority as she sat back and enjoyed her cup of tea. She was right. I was a stand up kinda nigga, and if my authority were challenged, I'd squash that shit. This situation was no different.

"Auntie, thank you for coming all this way, but a simple phone call would have sufficed. I hear your concerns and as valid as they may seem, if you knew I would react this way then you also know that there is nothing you can say to change my mind. This here is what made me the leader of this family. This ability to keep shit in line is what the board admired about me. It's what gives you, the board and them niggas that are loyal confidence in me.

Auntie, the board, put me in this position because I've always put the needs of the family first. So I don't mean this with any disrespect, but I already have your blessing. So don't ask me to sit here and allow some niggas, family at that to shit on us and our legacy. You know I'm not built like that. I love you, and I respect your advice and the advice of the board. But them niggas in the south need to know we mean business, and fucking with the FAM is bad for business and I'm going to make my presence known." I spoke as I stood and kissed her goodbye. I picked up the order of croissants I placed before heading over to the table. I exited the Cafe and made my way back across the street. I had been handed the keys to the kingdom.  It was time for me to flex my authority and make my presence known and felt throughout my domain. The King was coming, and the charge was war.

# "Hail Mary"

**- Tupac**

**Yazz**

Monica and I had been on assignment ever since I got that call from Jay. We had a time-sensitive issue to monitor and time was about up. I was on my way to scoop up Monica, and we were headed toward the stash house that was hit. Jay and Mario had figured out some shit and had sent me in to make sure things were working out. While they were out of town, Jay had me tighten things up. This meant I would be making steady appearances throughout the city. I monitored the drop houses, waited for the pickups, rolled up on the corners and even had the codes changed per Que. I had learned enough from Detroit not to ask questions. If work needs to be done, I was to do it. And this girl was ready to put in work.

I rolled up to Monica's crib just as some nigga was leaving. She quickly jumped in the car, and we headed out. We had a plan all in place. Today was the day. There would be no mistakes on our part. If there was anything I had learned, we were to be prepared, and there was nothing more dangerous than two bitches with attitudes. Oh yeah, today would be a good day I thought to myself. Monica was blazin' and nodding her head to the music that was blasting from the custom sound system I had installed. The bass that bumped through the speakers mimicked the sound of my heart. It was hard, intentional and calculated; it set the tone for today's events. It was soothing, calm and deadly. It was me on a mission. I joined in nodding my head as Tupac's "Me and My Girlfriend" blasted through the car.

We arrived at the spot. We stepped out of my Alfa Romero like top prize trophies. I was dressed in black leather pants and a crisp white crop tank top. My black peep-toe stilettos arched my back and made my ass pop. My hair was pulled back in a sleek ponytail. Monica had on a white pair of leather shorts and a black sheer long sleeve blouse that was tied in a knot on her right side. Her shorts barely covered her ass but showed off her curvy waist and her thick thighs. She had on a pair of floral print stilettos and carried a matching clutch. Everyone knew who we were. They could look, but we were off limits. No cat calls, small talk or long glares or that was your ass. We made our way past a few soldiers that were posted outside and those walking the street. I made my way to the back office. Monica and I went straight to business. Counting money and double checking inventory. One by one, each of the niggas in the house made their daily activity report to us. After the house was robbed, Mario had them report in daily.

Jay had Mario switch up the house members. He brought in other soldiers from other parts of the city to mix things up. But there were some who stayed. Mark, Ant, and Toke were three from the original team. They had been with the FAM for a while, had risen through the ranks. I knew these niggas went along with the new order of things, but they weren't happy about it. At each check-in I had everyone turn in their pagers and would hand out new ones. This was a system of checks and balances Que put into place. It was a way to make sure we knew who was talking to who. And since there seemed to be some trust issue, Que left no tables unturned.

It was about 6:30 pm and almost everyone had checked in with their daily reports. But as usual,

Mark, Ant, and Toke were pushing it, check in time ended at 7 pm., the pick for the house was at 7:15 pm. It was Saturday, and yes business always picked up around the weekend, but these three muthafuckas were trying my patience. Monica had paged in a crew from the fruit belt to come to the house; they were in route. We had been given the proceed code by Jay earlier today, so things were already set in motion. I was just waiting for these three assholes to grace me with their presence.

# "Get At Me Dog"

**- DMX**

## Mario

I just Scooped Que up from the airport. We were heading to the spot to meet up with the rest of the crew. I can't say I'm surprised to see Que; my big brother was always hands on. I did not expect anything less than him being here on the front line. He was quiet; I knew he was in deep thought. We drove in silence. I knew that Que preferred to drive in silence so he could keep a clear mind and focus. Besides, we were heading into battle, and the King needed to be on point.

We arrived at the meeting spot. Que got out the truck and was greeted by his army of loyal soldiers. Many of whom he had an appointment and handpicked himself. Que was calm, spoke his peace and went straight back to the office. I followed suit. Que was wearing a dark navy suit. It was hot as hell, and I knew he would need something a little more comfortable for the speed of the day. Once I had heard that he was on his way, I sent "B" and Tre' to the mall to cop some more appropriate clothing for Que. He went into the bathroom and changed. He reappeared like a street god. Wearing the Black jeans, tee shirt, and Black Timberlands. He had on his signature chain and Rolex. It was crisp and street clean. He opened his duffel bag and grabbed his NY fitted cap in black, and the outfit was complete.

"Is everything in place" Que asked. "Yeah" I replied. "We locked and loaded and ready to roll out" I continued.

"Good. let's get this shit done" Que said sternly walking out the back room and into the crowd of trigger happy niggas.

We drove the 30 minutes to the park. It was on the other side of town. We had 30 soldiers already posted up around the park. They gave us the intel that told us when all the key players were present. By the time we would arrive, the celebration would be ready to begin. We rode into the park and followed the directions that were given to the location of the family gathering. We could see about 100 cars and a pavilion full of country ass niggas skinnin' and grinin'. Most importantly we could see the heads of the territory for South Carolina. As we rode in the various cars split as we had planned, it was game time, and we were ready to get this party started.

# "Dangerous"

**- Busta Rhymes**

**Jay**

We had about an hour before game time. I never went into battle hungry and knew that the soldiers riding with me could use some substance. We headed out toward this joint called Miami Subs. It was off Skibo ave., and that street would take us to Raeford road which is where we wanted to be. I ordered a few subs for the crew. The honey behind the counter taking my order was cute. I could tell she was tryna' to get at your boy, but there were no takes. She was cute, but could not compare to Yazz. And as soon as this shit was done, I was heading back home to my baby. Besides, I didn't feel right asking her to pull off the job I gave her without me being there. Not that I didn't think she could handle it, but she had already been through enough. I paid, and them niggas ate; it was time to ride.

We pulled up to the motel off of Raeford Rd. It was a true hole in the wall joint, but it was perfect for a secluded meeting and what would happen next. We were about twenty cars deep, and to my calculations there should be about 70 people on the premises, not including hoes and bitches they might have brought with them. My crew had staked out all the homes of the individuals that would be in attendance. The order was clear and no one, and I mean no one was to be left alive. I had made arrangements prior with the desk person on site. The deal was simple, take the cash and get lost or die in the crossfire. She chooses option one, but not before I took her driver's license as proof that if she opened her big ass month, I would not hesitate to put my gun down her fuckin' throat. She nodded in fear, taking the suitcase full of money and quickly exited. She drove off and did not look back.

My Team had done their due diligence before today. The motel clerk had shown us that the surveillance equipment for the motel was outdated and barely worked. We made sure to permanently disable the system. We also surveyed the area, and no other businesses had systems that could capture any activity our way. So I was confident that when it came time to make a move, we were free and clear to act without worrying about being captured on film. It was game time. The clock read 6:58 pm and we were all in place. Without hesitation, I gave the signal. My crew and I surrounded the joint. It was going down, and I'd be damned if I let Que and the FAM down.

# "You Remind Me of Something"

### - R. Kelly

**Aaron**

Last day of freedom. I still can't get a hold of Anika. Ma probably mad at me for something, I'll fix all that when I get home tomorrow. But tonight, I'm going to scratch this itch I got. Lawd knows I try to be a good man, but if God wanted me to behave he wouldn't put all these temptations within my reach. Just then the doorbell rang. I had my towel wrapped around my waist; my dick rose with the excitement of what was waiting for me on the other side of the door. I open the door and just as I recalled, there he stood. He was Dominican, butter pecan complexion, petite and cute. We made eye contact at the restaurant the other night. I could tell that he was a full-fledged sissy. I could always pick them out in a crowd. He blushed, and I knew I had him. When I left the restaurant, I left a note for him at the hostess station, and like clockwork, this bitch is standing right in front of me.

We did not waste any time. He removed my towel and grabbed hold of my cock and massaged it like he owned it. He wrapped his lips around my cock and in the front room inhaled my massive piece. It was the itch I needed to be scratched, ever since my first encounter in college I knew, no one sucked dick better than a sissy. I was a college jock, and one night after a game I was approached by this older kid. I thought he was a fan and just really loved football. We were at the bar and drinks were following. We kicked it; I thought he was cool. We both were headed back to our respective dorms. I thought nothing of it; he was cool peeps. That was until in the dark of the night near a patch of bushes and trees; this muthafucka asked if he could suck my dick. At first, I wanted to punch him for asking me something like that. But before I could say anything, this nigga was on all fours with my cock in his mouth. I was mad and disgusted, but I could not pull away. The way he took me in and caressed me was nothing short of perfection. It was honest and pure and damn near sexy. I stood there dominating him. My cock in his mouth and eventually my cum all over his face. When we were done, he smiles and walks away as I stood there wishing that it had never happened.

No, I'm not gay! But, I love sex, and I'm down for anything that makes me bust a nut. It's the high I need and the feeling I desire all the time; it's my drug. And in the beginning, all it was, was him sucking me off until he wanted me to dominate him. I thought that was going too far. I hadn't even fucked a girl in the ass yet, how was I going to take this leap. But his touch and the warmth of his mouth made me excited, and before I knew it, my beef was pounding his flesh. He was tight. And no matter how hard I pounded that ass, he took it. I could not break him. He loved it, and I loved the challenge. After that night, my secret was born. I had found another way to satisfy my sexual craving. I have all the money I could want and a life many would kill for, and all I want right now is to dominate this sissy, I thought as he sucked my dick and made all kinds of joyous sounds.

I itched, and he scratched as I tilted my head back and closed my eyes and enjoyed the ride. I'm not sure what happens next or how it happens, but I raised my head to notice that the door was wide open and there stood a guy with a camera. The flash prevented me from seeing a face. I'm not sure how long he had been there, but I know for sure, that this shit cannot get out. No one could know about this, not my teammates, not my boys, and especially not Anika, I thought as I pushed the sissy to the floor and covered myself. Before I could question what the fuck was going on, the man with the camera was gone. I ran after him, but it was too late. Someone had proof; my dick went limp. How could I bust a nut after this shit?

# "Me and My Girlfriend"

-Tupac

## Yazz

I sat there in the office as these three niggas walked in as casual and nonchalant as a Sunday stroll. These niggas must not know I got the ear of the head and hand of the FAM. They tryna' play me like some weak as a bitch; I thought to myself as I watched them approach. They were gigglin' and shit like they just left the comedy club. I could tell they were caught off guard by the few changes that I had made. Earlier today Jay had ordered changes to the soldiers that manned the stash houses. Not just this house but all of them. Jay wanted to break up the inner clicks and make sure that he paired youngins with old heads. He said it kept it fresh, kept people moving, and would flush out anyone who was not loyal to the cause, plus considering that this house had rats, it was time to exterminate and eliminate. If there was one thing I knew about Anika's family Loyalty was everything. If you weren't loyal and your word wasn't law, than your rep was nothing. And the last thing needed in your crew was a weak ass nigga.

"Yo Yazz, wuzup with the new faces? Where's everyone at?" Mark spoke up. I could sense irritation in his voice. "These niggas looking me up and down like they don't know who the fuck I am." He added. Marked made his way to the office. Following right behind him was Toke and Ant. It was like a bad game of following the leader, and this nigga was leading them into a hail storm. Monica was seated on the back couch. She was the only familiar face in the room next to mine. I could tell these niggas was nervous, the giggling stopped. I think they could tell from my demeanor and the look on my face I did not have time for their fuckery today.

"Nigga you got my money?" I asked not crackin' a smile. I sat back in the chair waiting. My hand down by my side itchin', patiently waiting to be scratched.

"Bitch I got yo money" Mark spoke up. Chest puffed up like he was irritated at my question.

"Who the fuck are you talking to Nigga?" Monica said jumpin' up off the couch.

Marks tone caught the attention to the soldiers who were standing outside the office.

I held up my hand to signal them to hold off. Ant and Toke stood there. Not in awe that this nigga swelled up at me but in silence as if they agreed with his attitude. I knew for sure he was the leader.

I sat there calm as Mark, Toke, and Ant emptied their stashes on the table. I signaled one of the new soldiers to come and count the money. And just like I thought they were coming up short.

"Do you wanna explain why yall three muthafuckas short on my cash" I asked looking them all in their eyes.

"Bitch ain't nobody short, That nigga can't count." Ant spoke with aggression.

I smiled. My hand resting calmly. Itching.

Monica annoyed spoke up again, "Yall bum ass niggas got one more time to say something stupid before I kick ya ass."

"Where the fuck is Mario and Jay? I'm tired of answering to some bitch" Toke uttered with confidence.

Again I signaled for the soldiers in the house to back off. I stood, as my hand grew ever more irritated that it itched and had not been scratched. I watched as these niggas had no clue or just didn't care. I looked at them one by one. The clock read 6:59 pm. I was patient enough, and as the last 30 seconds ticked by, the itch became unbearable. I could hear them talking shit, Bitch this and bitch that, what you gonna do tell Jay I called you a bitch, I heard as they laughed and giggled at the pleasure of insulting me and my perceived weakness. The clock counted down as the third hand of the clock made its final approach to 7 pm. 9,8,7,6,5,4,3, 2,… BANG went the sound of my .45, BANG it went off again, BANG, BANG, BANG! Damn just like that; the itch was gone.

"Damn Bitch!" Monica yelled as she stood there looking at the three niggas that marched in here all cocky and shit, now lay helpless, lifeless on the floor of the office. Their blood flowed like a fire hydrant spraying the street on a hot summer's day. Only this time there was no children laughing and playing. Only the sounds of chaos and vengeance echoed as I walked over to them and fired off three more rounds. One for each of them; straight to the dome; blood splattered everywhere. By now the sounds had caught the attention to the crew in the house as well as the soldiers on the street. I stood there and admired my work. It was a job well done. Monica was pulling on me to go. She knew we needed to clear the house and move fast before the cops came. But I could not move. It was something about killing a person that made me smile on the inside. Like knowing I have the power to give and take life made me high. With every bullet I fired, I came alive. It was empowering, invigorating and downright therapeutic.

As I walked through the house, everyone's eyes were on me. I had bossed up.

Even though they knew me, everyone there now knew what I was capable of. I was not just Jay's girl, but I was part of the FAM, and I had rightfully claimed my role. They all knew it, and now they knew why. Everyone was given orders on where to meet up. The money at the stash house had already been moved earlier that day. I also had the crew remove any surveillance equipment, videos, and other items off the premises earlier too. The house was clean. All except the three niggas that lay on the floor of the office and their freshly painted blood that colored the paneling on the walls. As Monica and I made our way to the front door, I gave the order to burn it down. It was part of the plan Que had laid out. His orders were precise. Nothing was to be left standing.

As Monica and I drove away, I could see the thick smoke covering the neighborhood and smell the scent of a fresh fire burning. My pager had gone off. It was the code that the other job had been taken care off. Que had ordered no one left alive. So along with Ant, Mark, and Toke, he ordered everyone close to them to be taken out too. It was a sign that no one, not a single muthafucka better come up against the FAM. Not even one of our own.

# "What's Beef"

**- Notorious B.I.G.**

## Mario

I t was game time. These muthafuckas had no clue today was the day to end it all. It was got damn shame that it had to come down to this. The game had niggas fucked up, thinking that disrupting the flow of money would go unnoticed. Money and power make enemies of leaders and killers out of men. My ass was no exception to the rule. Once you got beef, you always have beef. Only way to squash conflict was to end those presenting conflict; I thought sitting in the Bronco getting ready to march on the killing field. We had been summoned to war, and as soon as the signal is given, I would soldier up and handle my business.

I looked around in the truck; we were all ready for battle. The silence was the deadliest weapon. Not knowing what a nigga is thinking, planning, the feeling was just as powerful as a bullet. All I knew, was the passengers in the truck with me were ready to die. They were loyal, and most importantly, they did not miss a target. As I looked out into the park setting, it was isolated. But if you aren't aware of your surroundings, you could easily ignore the obvious. The Family was so preoccupied with the smell of food, music and their treasonous acts; they didn't even notice, the soldiers hiding in plain sight. The signal had been given. And as swift as the breeze hit the trees, I had cocked the gun. Bullets flow to the sound of AK 47's, .45's, sawed-off shotguns, AR-15's like a chorus of guns singing a joyous song of vengeance. Bodies fell, young, old, men and women. Sadly, little children were caught in the crossfire. No time to mourn the loss of innocence born into life to crime.  Better them now vs. me in 10 years when they seek to act on behalf of their fallen loved ones.

The beef was never welcomed. But the sound of my gun clip emptying was as therapeutic as a good fuck. And defending the FAM's honor was my badge and duty.

# "We Don't Give a Fuck"

### - DMX

## Jay

The clock had struck 7 pm. I gave the signal, and the battle had begun. Soldiers rushed in guns blazin'. All you heard was the loud echoes of bullets piercing bodies. I stood back waiting for the all clear. The building had been secured. I entered the room where the family members were seated. A cloud of smoke and stench of gunpowder filled the air.  To their surprise, I stood in front of them. Their arrogance had them believing that Que and the Fam were clueless to their actions, but the look on their faces said it all.

It was too late to beg for forgiveness. These bitch ass niggas knew, I could, better yet Que could care less about someone crying and pleading for life. All those still breathing, kneeling, shook, knew what was coming next. It gave me no greater joy than to walk that line and pull the trigger. These were niggas I once considered family, now foes. Niggas that used to be my dawgs, thought had my back, all along plottin' and schemin' for my spot. The time for pleasantries was over.

One by one the power bestowed on me cast nothing but death. With every pull of the trigger, one shot to the head. Clean, effective. Death never looked good, but I made it picturesque. Like I had painted the walls in a beautiful abstract painting. One worthy of hanging in the NY Metropolitan Museum or the Louvre in Paris. The beauty of death was also ugly. Taking life was nothing short of playing God, but only a God would allow such a wicked act to provide such solace, peace, and grace.

POP. POP. POP. With my final shot, eight who once stood so cocky, now lay lifeless over a careless act. And for what? Their actions not only cost them their lives, but everyone they loved in one quick sweep, everyone was gone. Young and old. Confirmation came from everyone, targets eliminated. The battle was complete. Waiting to hear the war was over. The victory was ours.

What the fuck were these bitch ass niggas thinking?

# "The 10 Crack Commandments"

-**Notorious BIG**

**Que**

Cornelius sat there cowering underneath the picnic table like a little bitch. Can't believe this nigga wanted to dethrone me!! I laughed so hard on the inside as I noticed his pee soaked shorts. Money and family never mixed, but when you born into a family empire, you supposed to be stronger as a unit. Most of us understood that, but it was that one percent that did not give a fuck about the rules. Cornelius and his weak as crew thought the rules don't apply to them. That with all the money and power we had within reason, it was just not enough for this muthafucka. A piece of me wanted to go back to when we were kids, and I could just punch Cornelius in the face and walk away. Like when we were younger, and he would come to hang out with us in the Fruit Belt in Buffalo. Even though he was slightly older than me, I always dominated. He was weaker than me in every way, so the fact that this clown thought he should sit where I sit, eat what I eat, and rest his head where I lay, had me trippin'.

"Get your punk ass up" I yelled annoyed. Cornelius crawled from underneath the table. He was shaking like a cold Buffalo day hit his coatless soul. I hated to see grown ass men cower. It was a trait I was happy to be born without. If you play in this game, you better be ready to die. And if you not smart enough to manage your part in this drug game, then expect to live a short life. You never hear about drug dealers retiring from the game. You get carried out and buried six under; dethroned. No money, no handouts, most just strung out trying to relive the golden years with stories that start with when I was, or back when I…either way, everyone's number gets called sooner or later and today Cornelius and the whole family in South Carolina had a date with death.

Cornelius stood there as he watched every single member of his, our family that chose to act against the FAM catch a bullet to the dome. His mother, father, aunts, uncles, cousins, his kids, and his girl. One by one I walked the line and pulled the trigger. With each bullet, with each step, that nigga cried. He begged for me to spare their lives. He even got down and pleaded for me to just kill him instead. "Nigga doesn't worry; yo turn is coming. I wanted you to see what your jealousy and treachery resulted in.

I got a bullet with your name on it" I stated as I loaded another clip into my gun. Without words, I finished the task I came for. One by one body dropped. It was what I trained for my whole life. Eliminate the fucking enemy, but no one ever said it would be your own family. With each shot fired, I had a flashback of a moment I had with each of my aunts or uncles, cousins that stood before me. Whether it was a Sunday dinner, a wedding reception, a kiss on the cheek or a game of craps, they were memories that I had cherished. Now my final account of them would be this. My heart hung heavy, but my arm kept going despite the sorrow I felt.

Cornelius was the last person standing. I had managed to kill 20 individuals. The rest was gunned down trying to run away during the initial blaze of gunfire that escalated to this point. There were bodies everywhere, and I was going to add one more to the pile. Cornelius was like a catty church woman spilling the beans and praying for forgiveness. Of which, neither interested me. This was not personal; it was business. It was something that had to be done; I could give 2 fucks about anything he was saying. He could have called my mother a whore, and it would not matter at this point. He was a dead man walking, and I was the judge and jury. And his sentence was death. With one final bullet, I had completed my task. I can honestly say, it was the most painful. Cornelius lay there blood streaming out his head, eyes wide open.

21 bodies in one day was a lot of heat to catch. Shiiid, I may have broken a FAM record. It was a badge of accomplishment I could never be proud of. 21 Kills. 21 Kills that will haunt me for the rest of my life.

# "Untouchables"

**-Eric B & Rakim**

**Monica**

"THAT SHIT WAS CRAZY" I yelled as we drove off. Yazz was driving as if nothing happened. "Bitch, you hear me?" I questioned. This was the first time I had ever seen Yazz out of character. She was supposed to be the one that walked the straight and narrow, but what I just witnessed, was pure uncut savagery. This bitch cold clipped three niggas like she was taking out the garbage, and now we are riding down the 33 expressway like it's easy on a Sunday Morning.

"Yazz, yo kid, you aight?" I asked facing her to see her reaction.

"I'm good. You good?" she inquired back with a puzzled look on her face.

"Yo, Ma, I'm fucking great! As great as I can be after watching my best friend go all Rambo n shit. Naw I'm fucking Great!! You wanna explain what the fuck happened back there? Since when did you become all gangsta? You handled that shit like it wasn't your first time. What the fuck happened to you?

She just remained quiet. She drove in silence. But the look on her face said it all. She had changed, but why? What happens to Yazz? You just don't go from fucking niggas that run the street, to pulling a job, with no in between. This shit is not adding up. I had so many questions, and now was not the time to ask. I could tell that Yazz was in no mood to talk, and based on what just happened, I'm sure this was something that either Que or Jay had her do.

We pulled up to the safe house. It was just one of many that spread out over the city. This safe house was masked among the homes that canvased the Delaware Park area. It's beautiful brick exterior anchored the big picture window that welcomed you to the front porch. The front door, a steel custom wood stained glass inlay with bars protected our world from intruders, but also added charm and curb appeal. It was beautiful, but also served a purpose. I was sure that the door was a special order, equipped with state of the art surveillance and a bullet proof / anti-breaking glass. Yazz parked in the garage. We walked up to the back door and with keys in hand she opened the door, and we entered. Yazz walked over to the hallway linen closet and tossed me a towel and washcloth.

"Use the shower upstairs. You'll find a bag of clothing for you to change into on the bed in the middle bedroom. Be ready to go in 20 minutes." Yazz demanded.

I obliged because I did not know where her head was at. For now anyway. But this bitch done lost her mind. I don't know what happened to Yazz, but I know I'm going to find out.

# "If I Ruled the World"

- Nas

## Que

I felt the weight of a thousand years hanging over me. It felt like the clashing of a rose against the waves on a rocky coastline. My soul is battling against Lucifer, God raising his arm for me to take hold but the gravity of the sins I've committed preventing me from taking hold and the heat of hell starts to overtake my mental state. I'm at war with no way out. I can't win, and I can't lose. There is no justice for what I have done, and there is no punishment that I can't endure worse than the trial and jury that I have placed on me. I know now that one day my grave will be marked like the crimes I have committed.

I see the faces and know the names of every man and woman that I aimed and pulled the trigger against. Friend or Foe. Some, one and the same, all racing across my mind in a loud echo of pain and tears.

I catch my breath as the stewardess ask me if I would like a drink.

"Sir what can I get you" she repeated.

Um... I'll have a whiskey straight. Can you make it a double?" I added

She smiled warmly and shook her head to acknowledge the request. All I could think about is what kind of man am I that would bring a child into this world, my world? All I know is the street life. A life of power, money, and death. Yes, Death. It's either you or them, and you better have good aim and an even better judgment of character, 'cause the dudes that run with you better have your back, or they will be the ones taking you out hungry for that top position. I live in a world where loyalty is rare, and betrayal is constant. And if you're lucky, you only end up with scrapes and a few bruises. But a nigga like me, happy ever after is just a dream and yet I want it. I want it with Anika and our seed. But not in this life. Not living like this. My conscience won't allow it.

This was the quickest flight. I barely remember boarding the airplane let alone exiting. I grabbed my leather overnight bag from the overhead compartment. I made my way off the aircraft and into the airport. I gathered my thoughts. I did not need my facial expression to convey the heartache and pain I felt from the day's activities. What was done is done. I can't change not one outcome from today, and last time I check, I was far from Jesus Christ so there will be no resurrections because my conscience and emotions got the best of me for a moment. Fuck that shit. It was business. Sometimes corporations have to make swift hard decisions. The business of the FAM was no different. I stand by the call I made, the bullets blasted, and the body count. It was a decision and a job only I could undertake. It was a burden I was born to carry, heavy and proud, it was mine alone.

I rode down the escalator of the Toronto Pearson Airport, to be greeted by a middle-aged white man dressed in the standard black suite and cabby hat holding a sign with my name on it. We made eye contact, and he politely took hold of my overnight bag and escorted me out to the black town car parked right outside the sliding doors. The whole ride back to the hotel, all I could think about was my seed and Anika. I hoped that I would be a better man for both of them, but the reality was I wasn't sure I even knew how. What I did know was I had better figure it out soon, because either life or the consequences of my actions would determine the answer for me.

# "Money, Power, & Respect"

**-LOX**

## Jay

So we got out of North Carolina with no issues. The cleanup at the park went as planned. We all met up at Auntie Rose's house in South Carolina. We needed to sit still for a few days. Two days have passed so far. There had been some news coverage regarding the shootings at both the park and the motel. Nothing major and most importantly no leads or suspects reported. I had managed to tie up a few loose ends. WE now had an inside lead at the news station and within the police department. Money talks and can create new allies when needed. I had called in a new team to keep the business running in North Carolina, they were setting up shop already and had already made the FAM's new presence known. This left me feeling comfortable to travel knowing everything had gone as planned; I would head out tomorrow from Charleston. Mario and his crew would make their way up to Michigan in a clean car and nothing but overnight bags with new clothes in them, just in case they got pulled over the story added up. My crew would be leaving out tonight. They were equipped the same way Mario's crew was. Nothing extra, no souvenirs, and no signs of the last few days activities. As promised, everyone would be heavily rewarded for their loyalty to the FAM. Without a word, everyone knew the code to the game. We would never speak of this day again or mention ever being in the area. It was the code of the streets, and the loyalty the FAM demanded. Our business was always in the house. We kept our mouths shut and our pockets full and these niggas thrived in this type of environment. It was all part of the game.

Que was the only one to leave right out. I told him that I would finish up business here and meet him back in Toronto. I knew Que. We were like brothers. I could see the pain in his face. This hit by far was the hardest thing we have ever had to do. But Que was not the type of nigga to wear his emotions on his sleeve, that shit would never happen. And while everyone else thought he was good, I knew. He carried the pain in his eyes. His jawline was hard, and he did not speak a word. His hands were steady, but I could tell he needed to hit something or someone. A man with no outlet, is a dead man walking. Que needed to get back to Anika and the baby. He needed focus. He needed to remember why we do what we do. It wasn't always about the money, but the people we provide for, the family behind the FAM.

I dropped him off at a hotel in town. Gave him an overnight bag, we dabbed each other up. Without a word we knew. It was business and in our world Business never sleeps. Even when the job calls for a little extra, we always needed to deliver. This was no different. And the fact that he did it himself showed the rest of the crew why he was appointed the new Don of the FAM. And without question, Que got, earned and has the respect of all those under him now. The legend was born today and fear against the FAM holds steady.

I just can't wait to get back home to Yazz. I needed to make sure she was ok. I know she said that she could handle things, but this was her first job since we got back to Buffalo. And she did it alone. I just want to make sure her head is right. This life takes a toll on you, and I did not want it to change Yazz anymore than it has already. Hell, this life changed me, so I know what it can do to Yazz.

# "It Ain't My Fault"

**- Silkk the Shocker**

**Yazz**

I know that Monica ain't gonna let shit go. That bitch likes the National Inquirer. She will crack the case with like her middle name is Nancy Drew. It was only a matter of time before she put two and two together, so I needed to come clean and fill her in on what's going on with me. Hell, it might even be therapeutic. I needed to get this shit off my mind and if anyone could understand Monica would. I thought to myself as we drove down Delevan Ave headed to Jefferson. I made the sharp turn down Jefferson Street. The only thing that would calm my nerves right now was some good home cooking. If I couldn't get it from my moms, and I wasn't going to cook, Gigi's Restaurant was the next best thing.

We pulled into the lot adjacent to the restaurant. The parking lot was full. This was not unusual for this time of day. According to the Benz, Lexus and the kitted out Bronco's or Explorers the ballers knew it was time to eat too. There were only two things that would take the soldiers off the blocks, food, and pussy. And sometimes that was one and the same. We stepped out with all eyes on us. I could pull the trigger and pull off a pair of stilettos without missing a beat. Something a hard lesson will teach you real quick. I was wearing a hot pink mini skirt with a white tee tied in the back with a knot that gathered just enough to show off my pierced navel. I had on a pair of floral printed stilettos that pushed my ass up and out that helped my mini skirt hug my curves in all the right angles. Monica was wearing a neon orange scoop neck mini dress with a pair of strappy white, orange and black heels that wrapped up around her legs and tied just below her knees. Both of us smelling like danger and fun all rolled up in one. It was the scent every man wanted to try.

We walked into the restaurant and took the last two-seater table located near the rear of the building. Niggas were all smiles: some with gold teeth, some missing teeth. I could see the rolls of money bulging in their pockets, but I think it was very clear by the head nods and stares that everyone knew who we were and who we were with. It was the power of the FAM and the fame that came with being the girl of Buffalo's finest.

The waiter came over and asked what he could get us to drink. We both ordered two large Loganberry drinks. Big momma came over and gave me a hug as soon as she saw it was me. Big Momma was a mom figure to every drug dealer and lost soul this side of Lake Erie. She fed us all, not just physical food, but knowledge and life lessons, especially when it seemed the streets was getting the best off us. Her hug was like a hug from my grandmother, welcomed and long overdue. She took our orders. She gave us a look as if to say was Jay and the crew coming, I just shook my head, and she smiled and moseyed back into the kitchen to get our orders.

Monica was quiet. I could tell she was trying to make the pieces fit the puzzle that is me. She rolled her eyes and just shook her head.

"Bitch I need to blaze," she said in a snotty tone. "I'm going to the car for a minute" she snapped. I let her sash shay her way through the crowd of mismatched tables and chairs.

Big Momma came back over to the table and took a seat.

"Where Monica going?" she asked.

"She needs some fresh air," I replied.

"That girl went outside to smoke a joint" Big Momma laughed letting out a good chuckle.

"We can't hide nothing from you," I answered

"Yazz" she called out my name while grabbing hold of my hand, "baby girl what is going on?" she continued. "And before you say nothing, I've known you since you were six inches long and pissing in diapers, so don't lie to me."

Her words touched me. It was like talking to my G-ma. I could feel the fears and tears swelling up in me. I could not look her in her face. My eyes would tell the pain and terror I've been through these past eight months. I had done a great job holding it in, and goddamnit I refuse to fall apart now.

"Before I lie to you, where my fried chicken at Big Momma?" I changed the conversations putting on a fake smile.

"Ok little girl. I's see you. Just don't hold that shit in too long. These streets ain't got time for someone who doesn't know right from wrong. And they damn sho don't get time for someone who can't figure out who the fuck they are." she spoke looking me dead in my eyes. "You want hot sauce with that chicken?" she added nonchalantly.

"Yeah, Big Momma. Bring that Frank's Hot Sauce to the table." I humbly replied.

Big Momma was right. I needed to get this shit off my chest. Not now but soon. And if Monica weren't acting so shitty right now, I would of….

Who the hell I'm tryna fool. I wasn't ready to relive that shit let alone break down in the middle of this restaurant full of niggas. I'll do it, just not right now.

Just then Monica came back into the restaurant, and our plates were heading out to the table. It was best we eat first. Monica wanted to know what was up with me. That bitch was gonna need all her strength a blunt and some Henny to get through all I was about to release on her. Eat up Monica, 'cause this shit will be the desert you been after and didn't even know you wanted.

# "Nigga What, Nigga Who"

**-Jay Z**

## Mario

It feels good to back in the city. Ain't shit like riding through your hood. After that bullshit down south, I was on a natural high. It felt good to be back where I did not have to flex on nobody, better yet, I did not have to worry about the next man. These streets already knew. There wasn't a corner, nigga, or bitch that did not know who and what I represented. I rode around just for show. Dudes would nod their heads as a sign of acknowledgment, chicks would clock my every move hoping to be my next victim. I had the bass bouncing from the amps in the trunk. My gear was always on point and my wrist shined like the sun. We were on top, and now that the FAM had established and re-established our claim, all was good for the moment, but as Que would say, money never sleeps, and any nigga sleeping deserves to get his money and spot taken.

I made my way through the territory to let all the street soldiers know that I was back. Honey turned their heads tryna catch a glimpse of me in my ride. They knew daddy was back. But there was only one person I want to see right now, Monica. I knew that she could set it off just right and welcome ya boy home proper.  But before I headed over to see Monica, I had some business to take care of. I finished my rounds, collected, visited a few peoples, and then headed over to the barber shop.

My Man Tree was one of the best barbers in the city. He kept my 360 tapers on lock. The tree was a Soldier in his own right. There were all kinds of traffic coming through the shop. From the mix tape sellers to the purse dude selling freshly stolen Gucci, Fendi and MGM purses, to the bootleg movies. Whatever you were looking for you could find it at the barber shop. Not to mention all the hotties, hoes and hoodrats that frequented the shop, so there was always some new pussy you could pick up and turn out just from getting your haircut.

I stepped up into the open the door to the barber shop. There was music playing, laughter, people waiting their turn for a fresh cut, and as always a conversation about the latest gossip in the city. Tree looked up and motioned me to come on over. There was never a waiting period, or an appointment needed.

"Hold up homie; I got you next Tree said to a slender older brother who thought he was next up to the chair. The dude took one look at me, nodded, lowered his head, and sat back down. A few dudes I knew came over and dabbed me up. Tree went right to work on making my 360 tapers crisp. I listened to the daily gossip and street banter. Keeping my ears to the street meant being able to weed out what was real from the fake news — knowing what was important to the flow of business vs. nonmuthafuckin' factors. You know crews that thought they could roam my streets looking for a quick come up. I could find all that out and then some by hanging out in the barber shop. It was amazing how lose niggas lips get when they tryna to inflate their street cred. Besides my man Tree would always let me know if there was anything he thought I should know before it hit the streets. He was a longtime ally of the FAM, and for that, he reaped the benefits of being part of the family.

As usually, my taper was on point as I checked out Tree's craftsmanship in the walled mirror that lines the wall of the barbershop. We dabbed up and agreed to get up later. As I was about to leave the shop, some nigga came in hyped up off something. The look in his eyes spoke nothing but trouble. The nigga walked past me, pulled out his gun with all the intentions to rob my man's spot. His loud eerie voice screamed above the beat of Jay-Z's Hard Knock Life. I turned to see him holding one of the young boys who was waiting to get a haircut. I quickly locked the door to prevent anyone from entering. I did not want anyone to walk into this situation and cause the gunman to act in panic.

"Yo, my man" I addressed the gunman. He turned panicky in my direction.

"Nigga what you want" he replied looking me in my eyes.

"What is it going to take to get you to let the little shorty go?" I placed my hand in my right front pocket. Pulling out a good sized knot holding it up I added, "You can have this knot, but you gotta let shorty go first."

I could tell by the excitement in his eyes that he was a hype. He was either cracked out or addicted to some other drug. Either way, the grin on his face told me all he wanted was some quick cash to get high on. He reached for the stash. I pulled it back.

"Let the kid go" I demanded.

I could hear the cries of his mother asking him not to hurt her son.

"Let the kid go" I repeated.

"Who the fuck are you to demand anything of me" he spoke waving the gun at me.

The barbershop stood silent. All the idle gossip and chatter came to a halt.

"You don't know who I am?" I asked.

The gunman looked puzzled. "Nigga if knew who you were, I wouldn't have asked" he stuttered.

"Would anyone like to tell him who I am?" I asked into the barbershop.

The young boy being held by the gunman spoke "that's Mario." as he looked up at the gunman.

"I don't give a flying shit about no Mario" the gunman laughed.

The little boy spoke again and whispered: "of the FAM" it was just loud enough for the gunman to hear, and loud enough that it grabbed his memory. The look on the gunman's face as he began to realize the consequences of his actions went from drugged out, to a quick sober.

"Let the little boy go" I spoke sternly.

Without hesitation, he released the little boy, who went running towards his mother.

The gunman placing his gun down on the coffee table that sat in the middle of the waiting area of the barbershop, slowly took a knee and started begging for forgiveness.

"Mr. Mario, I'm sorry. I-I-I didn't know this was your place. Y-Y-You se-e-e, I'm sick off that shit. Som-m-me times it plays wit' my mind, and I-I-I can't think straight. I didn't mean no harm." he stuttered

Tree quickly grabbed the gun. I stood there looking at this worthless piece of shit. I wanted to blast his ass for rolling up in here and disrespecting everyone, but I knew killing him in front of all these people was not the best way to handle the situation.

"Tree call for a car to come and help clean up this situation" I spoke as I could see Tree was already on it.

I could see the gunman crying and praying as he was anticipating my next move. I could also feel the eyes of everyone in the barbershop on me, both young and old. All are waiting and wondering what was next.

I walked over to the now cowardly gunman, I squatted down to his level, whispered in his ear so that only he could hear. His eyes got big, and he nodded his head in approval to everything I said. I could tell that he knew I meant business. From the tone of my voice and my calm demeanor, he knew that I was not playing. I ended our conversation with "do you understand?", he answered "Yes" in a childlike voice. "Did I make myself clear?" I added, "Yes" he added shaking his head in agreement. I stood up, to noticed that he had pissed himself during our conversation. Disgusted, I stepped away from him. Grabbed a roll of paper towels that were sitting on the ledge by the barber station, threw them at him so that he could wipe that shit up. Right on time, a car had pulled up at the back of the shop. Two young crew members walked in through the backdoor. Without so much a word, the gunman got up and walked toward the two men, and out the back door, they went. I smiled at the young man who was being held by the gunman. He ran up to me and hugged my leg. I rubbed his head and gave him dap as his mother whispered, "Thank You." I looked at Tree shaking my head and said: "I'll catch you later god" as he nodded in agreement. Unlocked the front door and made my way out the shop.

# "Phone Tap"

## The Firm ft. Dr. Dre

**Aaron**

Where the fuck is Anika!! I've been home now for 2 days, and I can't find her. The last thing I need is for something bad to happen to her. Hell, it was bad enough that I need to find out who is after me. I can't stop thinking about what happened. Who knew about my secret? I was always careful about protecting my extracurricular activities. I was careful about who I choose, the where, and when. Everything was at stake. My career, my reputation, and Anika. 'WHERE THE FUCK IS SHE?!" I screamed into the empty house taking another sip of Hennessy straight from the bottle.

My mind was playing games on me. I started thinking that the house phone was tapped. Or maybe I was being followed. But who would do something like this and why? A million thoughts crossed my mind, none of them good. I haven't slept soundly since that night. All I keep seeing is the image of a person in the doorway of the hotel and the flash of a camera going off. Shit!! How am I going to be able to explain this to Anika? She'll never understand. She'll leave me and take our baby I thought as tears began to form in corners of my eyes. How did I get here? Why can't I control these urges? What the fuck is wrong with me? I sat there at the kitchen table wondering how my life could take such a turn. I have everything, and it wasn't enough. I have a girl that loves me and is carrying my baby, a career and a life anyone would trade theirs for. And now, with those pictures out there, all that can end. But why? Why would anyone want to take that away from me? I had to find out why. Who? Before Anika finds out. I took the last sip of Hennessy, got up from the table and headed to the bedroom.

I took a quick shower, got dressed and out the door. I knew where I could find Anika, Monica would know where she is at. I rode the Interstate 33 into Buffalo. Took the Suffolk to exist and in about 10 minutes I was at Monica's. She had moved a few months back, and I remembered dropping Anika off at her new spot. I have to admit, Monica was the kind of chick I would normally fuck. You know the nasty freak like a girl that you have fun with and leave when you done, but I knew with how close Anika and Monica were, I had better not try to fuck both of them. But, the stories dudes be telling about Monica had a nigga wondering.

I turned on Monica's street. Pulled up in front of her house. There was a Maserati parked in the driveway. I wondered what poor soul she had wrapped around her finger this week. I rang the doorbell. The door opened, and I was greeted by Monica in a not welcomed manner.

"What the fuck you want?" she started.

"Hello to you too. I'm looking for Anika, is she here?" I asked trying to pull on the locked screen door.

"Bitch if you don't stop trying to break my door.." Monica sternly stated looking me in my face.

"Look I know she's here, let me see her." I pleaded.

"Aaron" Monica said laughing. "Anika is not here. Maybe if you kept your wondering ass home, you would know that" she added.

"Bitch look, tell Anika I'm out here, and I need to see her. I demanded.

"I told your dumb ass already she not here. Now get the fuck off my property." Monica spoke up in a loud ghetto rhythm.

"Then where is she? I know you know. I checked her mom's house and her grandmothers; you're the only other place she would be. Monica please, I just need to make sure she's ok." I pleaded one last time.

Monica stood there laughing. I wanted to punch the shit out of her.

"Yo, this nigga think that I'm going to tell him where Anika at." she jokingly spoke looking back into the house.

"If she wanted you to know, you'd know. Or better yet, maybe it wouldn't have taken you so long to figure out she's been gone for weeks." a sarcastic voice uttered from behind the door.

"Who the fuck are you? You don't know shit about me and Anika" I firmly stated

Just then the door opened, and there stood Yazz. She stood there with a devilish grin and a no-nonsense look on her face.

"Nigga, I know enough to know that you don't know where yo girl at and I do. And if she wanted you to know she would have told you.

Now get the fuck on like Monica asked." Yazz spoke.

"Bitch both of yall need to tell me where she at before I.

"Before you what?" Yazz said, opening the screen door and flexing the .45 that rested in her hand. "Before what, you were saying..?" She continued.

All I could do was take a step back. My hands were in the air as to surrender the conversation.

"Look, ladies, I just want to see Anika, please just tell me where she's at or better yet tell her to call me. Please!" I begged.

They both just laughed in unison. I could feel the anger build deep within me, but I kept my cool. One thing's for sure; I thought as I headed back to my car, if Yazz and Jay were back, then Que can't be that far behind. I'd have to deal with that thug nigga another time, right now the question remains, who the fuck is out to get me? I need to talk to Anika quick before everything falls apart.

# "5 Miles to Empty"

## - Brownstone

## Anika

I had spoken to my mom. She told me that Aaron had stopped by looking for me. I had already told her where I was and with whom. I can't say she approved, but I knew she trusted my judgment, and right now I wasn't sure if that was such a good thing. Being that I'm carrying one man's child and engaged to another, doesn't speak much of my judgment. I had told my mom that if Aaron had stopped by or called not to tell him anything. I needed time to figure things out, and considering my current state, I did not need any added stress. I could only handle one issue at a time.

I was torn and torn between two men. One I knew could love me and give me the life I always thought I deserved: the other, my first and only true love. I could not live in his world, because I could never be first. The constant danger, not to mention he is the father of my child. Is that really how my child should grow up? Am I already being a victim of the streets, a statistic? I knew I only loved one, but I could learn to love the other. Either way, I needed to make a decision and soon. I know Que will be back any minute. He called to tell me he would be back later tonight. A day later than he initially said. That was fine. It gave me another day to rest and hopefully get my life in order. Damn girl, what are you going to do? I thought silently to myself looking out the windows of the penthouse admiring the scenic views of downtown Toronto.

"Girl, that nigga showed up at my house looking for your ass. It took all I had not to tell him you were with Que" Monica bragged.

"Thank you for not telling him, Monica. I'll call when were done." I replied.

"Yo, Sis, don't even sweat it. Take your time. That baby and your health come first, don't be working yourself up over some nigga, Que included." Monica added.

"You right Mo. But I gotta face this shit sooner than later. I got myself into this shit; I'm grown enough to admit and confront this head on. The doctor said that I'd be ready to travel back home as early as tomorrow. I'll call you as soon as we get there." I stated trying to change the conversation.

"You ain't slick bitch," Monica laughed, but ok. I'll see you soon. Please, we need to talk about Yazz." Monica continued.

"What about Yazz?" I asked.

"I'm not going to worry you right now; we'll talk soon." Monica insisted.

"Cool. Love you Mo." I ended the conversation.

"Love you back Bitch" Monica finished and hung up the phone

"Hello, Aaron. I know that you're home. I've been trying to catch you. I've left messages at the hotels and with...." the message was quickly interrupted by picking up of the telephone.

"Anika! Where are you, baby? I've been looking everywhere for you. Are you ok? Is the baby ok? Where are? Aaron spoke in one breath.

"beep" went the answering machine.

"Aaron, I'll be able to explain everything to you soon. I just want to let you know that I'm ok. The baby is fine." I spoke softly.

"Anika where are you?" Aaron asked.

I could tell there was a sense of fear in his voice. I could only imagine what he has been going through.

"Aaron, I don't want you to freak out. I'm in Toronto. I came up here and got sick and haven't been able to leave." I replied.

"Why didn't your mom tell me when I asked her? Did she not know? What about Monica and Yazz? Why did they keep this from me?" Aaron demanded to know.

"I asked them to. I just needed time" I whispered with a heavy heart

"Time for what Anika?" Aaron asked sternly.

"Aaron, I told you we could talk when I get home. I just can't right now" I spoke.

"Wait for a minute damnit; you're carrying my child; we're engaged, I demand to know!" Aaron yelled into the phone.

"I'm not doing this with you, Aaron. I just wanted to call you and let you know; I'm ok. We can talk in 2 days when I get home." I spoke up. I could feel the tears in my eyes starting to form. I just couldn't continue the conversation. "Good Bye" I continued and hung up the phone.

I sat there holding my now well-developed belly. How could I not tell him that the baby was not his? How could I lead him on like this? He is such a good man. How will he ever forgive me? How will I ever forgive myself? I cried just thinking of the pain and heartache I was about to cause. Loving one man that could not love me back and keeping him from knowing he's the father of my child or not telling the other he is not the father and allowing him to love me knowing I can't love him the way he deserves, either way, it's a fucked up game I've played. And I may be the one person that ends up losing. All I could hear was my Dad whispering "Checkmate." How disappointed he must be looking down at me. Playing a game, I could not win was never a strategy he taught me. FUCK!

# "Till the Cops Come Knockin"

— **Maxwell**

**Que**

Being with Anika gave me solace. I could just be me. It was my reprieve from the rest of this world I lived in. I wanted to love her, love her the way she deserved to be loved. To make a life, she would be proud of for her and my seed. I wish I could wash my hands of this life I live, but I can't. I'm stained with the blood and crimes of the FAM. And after this last job, I'm not sure there will ever be a time I could just leave it all behind. I thought as I rode the elevator up to the penthouse suite. The bell rang to announce my arrival. The doors opened.  There she sat at the dining room table. She was the most beautiful woman I'd ever known. I wanted her from the first time I saw her. And now we are forever connected. I walked over to her and kissed her gently on the forehead. She looked deep in thought. Anika rose to hug me. I embraced her in my arms and could not let go. I held her like a summertime memory in the winter cold.

She was just what I needed. My medicine from the cruel world I walk in and the peace of mind I craved. I picked her up. She smiled. I kissed her lips as I carried her into the bedroom and closed the door. I placed Anika gently on the bed. She undressed me and me her. It was the first time since I left her that I was going to enter my sanctuary. I wanted to worship her and have her wash away my sins. She lay back on the bed. I had imagined every curve of her body. I knew every mole, scare, and scratch on her. They were landmarks that I had kissed over and over in my mind, and her I was to indulge in all the fantasies that I dreamt over the last eight months. She glowed as the light from the sky line cascaded down on her through the blinds of the wall to wall windows that line the bedroom. I wanted her; I was addicted to her. Her scent, her smile, her laugh, I wanted it all to myself. They were the pills I needed daily to keep living I thought as my tongue made its way up one leg and down another.

My manhood was fully erect as she climbed on top of me. I was scared that I would harm the baby, but Anika assured me it was ok. I sat there as she straddled me, holding on to her waist as she glided up and down. I kissed her enlarged breast and belly as she let out moans and sighs of pleasure. Her pussy was extra wet and soft. I held on as she rode me and reminded me why I fight so hard. Why I would die protecting her and my seed. I lost control of my thoughts and feelings as she rode slowly and gently to a steady rhythm. It was the everything I needed and everything I didn't know I could have. I could feel my toes curl and crack as she gave me my blessings. It was the eight months welcome home I had anticipated — a party made for two.

I turned her over on her right side and penetrated her from the back. It allowed her to rest and gave me a chance to return the favor. She wrapped on leg around my thigh and allowed me to run my hands up and down her clitoris as my dick pushed deeper and deeper into her. She moaned for me not to stop. I could feel her sweet juices dripping out of her as I gave her all of me. It washed me and made me whole. It was my strength and approval I needed. Anika's moans told me how much she missed me; I knew she still loved me. With every pump, she thrusts back at me. I knew I was what she needed also. With both our bodies wet and the clapping of my thighs against her booty, the screams of satisfaction and the constant streams of pleasure running down my dick, told me I was home. Safe and Sound.

Anika grabbed my rock hard dick and stroked me into her mouth. I looked down at her as she her perfectly pink lips surrounded my dick as she took me in and out. She licked up and down my shaft, stroking me as I lost control and my body shook to her will. She was gentle yet forceful. I could tell she wanted me to explode. I sat on the edge of the bed as she sucked, stroked, stroked and sucked me into heaven. And without hesitating, she opened her mouth to welcome my long-awaited arrival. I could see from the light of the skyline as I exploded in her and on her. My cum dripped off her lips, down her neck, and onto her breast. She sat there bathing in my eternal gratitude. She had been everything I ever wanted and everything I needed. I watched as she drank what she could and gently massaged me into her. She stood and presented herself to me. We embraced, and I kissed my seed resting inside her. It was the peace and contentment only she could provide. It was what I longed for. It was one of the few times I allowed myself to be vulnerable. I knew at this moment Anika, and I would be together forever, that I could keep business and family life separate. I had too. I just had too.

# "You Got Me"

**- The Roots**

**Jay**

Mario told me about the minor situation he had to diffuse at the barbershop. I was impressed with how he used restraint. In his earlier years, we would have been picking up a body and sending in a cleanup crew. The kid is showing growth and maturity. He was starting to think like Que and me. What would Que and Jay do was always a good question to ask when some shit goes down. Other than that, everything had been good since we got back. I've been keeping an eye out on any news from the situation down south. So far nothing. It was still circulating in the news but no real leads, no witnesses and nothing they weren't reporting before we left. Everyone made it back without any problems. I had the Detroit crew checking in, and the new crews in South and North Carolina stated it was business as usual. Auntie Rose even chimed in and said the streets were back to normal. It was a new era for the FAM. With Que at the head of the organization, I was positive that he could take this street game to the next level. Further, he could end the bullshit and the bloodshed.

I had one day before Que brought Anika home. He left specific instructions. He had more surprises in store for her than a 5-year-old's birthday party. I knew my brother had enough on his plate. Dealing with business and trying to do right by Anika and the baby was a lot. Hell, I could barely keep Yazz and me straight, throw in a baby, and that would be a game changer. I hadn't had time to be with Yazz now unless it was business related. This was something I needed to change. It seemed that Yazz had changed her mind about the street game. At times she seemed more into it than me. I wanted out or at the very least an exit strategy. Seemed like she was all in. It was scary how one fucking event can change a person. My good girl was gone. I just hope the monster I helped create could be tamed. I hoped my love for her would be enough to see us through to the end.

I had finished up business and had headed home. Yazz said that she would meet me there shortly. She said that she and Monica were finishing up something and she would fill me in later. I was cool with that. I thought I'd do something special for Yazz to remind her that it's not always about business. It may be what brought us together in the beginning, but it was my inner charm and character that made her fall in love with me.

I quickly jumped in the shower and cleaned off the day's dirt.  I put on a new outfit I had picked up while in New York City on my last visit with Brothers. I sprayed on some Polo cologne, and I was ready for my baby to come home. I headed toward the kitchen and tried to figure out what can I cook up for a romantic evening home.

Ever since we got back to Buffalo from Michigan, I had wanted to cook dinner for Yazz in our new home. But things happen so fast with a business that I just didn't have the time. But tonight was the night. I immediately began toasting some fresh herbs, shallots, and garlic. The whole house smelled of deliciousness. I took the porterhouse steaks and placed them on the indoor grill and allowed the juices and spices to smoother the house. I had roasted potatoes that were tossed with olive oil and the toasted herbs. And finally a green salad with beets, feta, and walnuts. Que would always try to clown me about my culinary skills. He said I was always gettin' the ladies by cooking for them. He was right. I would cook, and they would drop those panties. But Yazz was different. She was someone I could see me waking up to every day. She was someone I could make waffles for and have Sunday breakfast in bed. She gave me hope. Yazz is the seasonings my life needed; I just wanted her to know that. And with perfect timing she would, I thought as I heard the back door open and could hear the steps of her stiletto shoes click along the tile floor leading to the kitchen.

"Hey pretty lady," I said as she entered the room. My grin on my face stuck in her presence. Yazz was the most beautiful woman I had ever seen. Everything about her was just right for me. She stood there wearing a blue tank style dress, that hugged her hips and thighs. It stopped four fingers above her knees. Short but not too short. She had on a thin gold chain necklace with a pair of gold large hoop earrings. She was wearing the Rolex I gave her and a host of gold bangles that jiggled when she moved. She walked right over to me and gave me my long-awaited hug. It felt good. It felt right. It felt like home. Plus she smelled hella good.

"Hey Papi" she spoke as we kissed. "You've been busy I see. It smells so good in here. Did you do this all for me?" She continued.

"Only for your love" I replied. Holding on to her by the waist.

"Let me get dinner on the table. Come sit down" I added.

"Do I have time to freshen up real quick" Yazz asked.

"Sure Ma, but don't keep me waiting too long. I haven't seen you all day." I replied.

Within minutes Yazz reappeared dressed in a sexy black lace one piece. It reminded me of some kind of body suit. Her body was bangin'. Her legs bathed in baby oil and her breast were situated perfectly high in the cups of the bodysuit. She looked amazing walking toward me in a pair of Christian Louboutin patent leather heels. She sat down at the dining room table. I placed the plates down and joined her. Her confidence and sexiness looked just as delicious as the food I had prepared; I wasn't sure which one I want to eat more. I allowed her to eat a few bites before my lust for her got the best of me.

I pushed my seat aside and walked over to her, picking her up and placing her on the table. I opened her long, lean legs and dove into the only meal I wanted. My tongue quickly found its way to my main course. She was sweet and juicy as I licked and sucked with every moan Yazz uttered. She twisted and turned as I licked her clit and gently pulled on it. I licked and inserted my tongue inside her. In and out, in and out my tongue drove as my fingers played her ass and breast like a guitar. She wiggled and sighed, as I loved her and ate my meal. I sexed her, and she thanked me over and over again as her sweet juice glided down my lips and onto my tongue. I wanted her. All of her and would not stop until she surrendered herself to me. My fingers played her ass as she began to ride them mimicking the way she rides my dick. I had stretched the opening of her ass to accommodate three of my fingers. It gave her the girth and length she needed to fuck me back. I held her pussy open with the other hand massaging her outer lips as my tongue spanked her clitoris. I sucked and lick. She bucked and rode. I massaged and spat, she screamed and held on, I licked and fingered, she moaned, twisted and turned. It was a battle only one of us could win. And finally, I could hear her breath quickening, and her body quivering. I looked up at her as she balanced herself on the table and was finally ready to give in to me. With locked eyes, she rode, and I thrust, licked and waited for her love to pour down into my deserving mouth.

Without losing a beat I turned her over, ripping the lace bodysuit off her exposing her sexy body. I dropped my pants and rammed my rock hard dick deep into her. Smacking her round ass, I fucked her like it was the first time she gave it up to me. She lay sprawled out on the dining room table like my buffet, and I had her any way I wanted. Right now my dick had her bouncing and bucking back at me as I entered her with force. She moaned and called out my name. It turned me on even more. And I wanted her even more. I pumped her as her ass shook. I held onto her waist and gave her every inch of my dick. She was my second course, and I was enjoying every moment of it.

# "I Can Love You"

**- Mary J Blige ft Lil Kim.**

## Monica

Mario would be here any minute. The house was clean, and a bitch even made dinner. The last thing I needed to do was finish my makeup, and I would be ready for whatever the night had in store. It had been a few days since I had seen Mario. All I knew was something BIG went down, and the crew headed out. I knew enough not to ask questions, the less I know, the better. Besides if I didn't know nothing, then I couldn't testify in court. But Mario's young ass was different. He was the right amount of thug and gentleman. He spoiled me. Not just with gifts but with the dick. He gave it to me how I needed when I needed it and even when I didn't need it. He had the charm of a school boy and the street smarts of a man twice his age. Plus he had a body. Mario was built as fuck. From his chiseled arms to his rock hard abs, he made me feel safe every time he held me. It was becoming additive. Look at me thinking about a nigga like I'm claiming him.

Would it be so bad if… if me and Mario we're exclusive? I mean damn, I've pretty much scaled back my list of niggas. I can't remember the last time I wrote a new victim in my little black book; we've been spending all our free time together anyway. I knew that he had gotten rid of that Carol chick. I wasn't sure if he had another side piece, but I know for sure can't nobody give it to him the way I can. It was all over his face when I put it on him. He already gave me keys to his place. Not that I would use them, but I had them, and that said a lot to me. Mario trusted me, and at times I wasn't even sure I could trust myself. Besides, Mario accepted me for me. He knew all about my past, the games I played, how I roll, and how I get my money. Not once did he try to change me. He knew and loved how gritty and grimy I could be and how I could flip the script and be ladylike, like Anika's stuck up ass. Maybe it wouldn't be so bad to be tied to just one nigga. Maybe it was time for this girl to do something different. I know one thing, daydreaming about a nigga ain't gonna finish this face, I thought as I outlined my lips and applied a slutty shade of red lipstick

Checking myself out in the mirror, I was ready. Mario's ass better hurries up and get here. Look at me, I blushed. This nigga got me open. His young ass got me feeling some kind of way. Is this what Anika and Yazz's asses go through? Them bitches know they will hold on to one dick forever. Be all wired up and shit. But I had to admit, Mario made me want that life, made me want to be his and only his. This is way out my comfort zone.

"Get your shit together' bitch," I said out loud while looking at myself in the full-length mirror. "Tonight is about fuckin', nothing else. Just me and that fine ass Mario fuckin." I continued. Catching feelings was not in the plan, and right now I need to stick to the plan.

# "Back that Ass Up"

- Juvenile

## Mario

I finally made my way to Monica's house. No need to ring the doorbell, she had already told me to just come on in. It was weird. I could remember a time when Monica wouldn't give me a second look, use to call me youngin'. She would flirt but wouldn't give ya boy a chance. And look at us now. She had a nigga feignin' bad. Had me addicted to her pussy, her vibe, and shit. Mo was the only thing I could think about other than business. Hell, I got rid of all them other hoes because there was no one that came close to how she made me feel. Plus, I needed to show her that I was serious. Monica was used to hangin' wit Ballers, literally. So if I was going to keep her interest long term, I had to pull out all the stops.

Because everything I knew about her, she would either dog the fuck out of a nigga or ride that dick until she was bored of you. I just didn't want to be that dude. My ego wouldn't allow that, so I had to come correct.

I walked into the house. You couldn't tell that Monica had recently moved in a few months ago, it was already fully furnished. There were knick-knacks and pictures already displayed around the house. I could smell seasonings that mimicked the cooking of spaghetti sauce and garlic bread. The lingering of a lit incense filled the air as I turned the corner leaving the kitchen into the dining room. There she sat with both legs propped on the table crossed wearing nothing but a pair of black strappy high heels and a smile that lit up my heart. She was puffing on a blunt looking sexy as hell.

"Hey Mo," I said smiling.

"Hey," she said walking over to greet me.

I was instantly turned on. She had a walk that would stop niggas dead in their tracks and body that would have any grown man wanting to touch. My dick was instantly hard at her presence. She kissed me, twisting her tongue in my mouth. The sweet taste grape from the blunt wrapper drove me into her. We kissed. It was hard, long and passionate. She stood there in her beauty, pressing her body close to mine. She grabbed my dick as it was begging to be freed from my jeans. She rubbed me gently and whispered in my ear "I need you now." This was the kind of shit I loved about her. She was straight forward, sometimes too straight forward. But right now it was just what I needed to hear.

Monica unzipped my jeans, and without so much, a word massaged my dick into her mouth. She welcomed me back from my trip as I had been gone for years. The stroke of her hand with the flickering of her tongue on the tip of my dick drove me crazy. She sucked and stroked and made me weak in my knees. Without asking she managed to persuade my body to sit on the chaise lounge chair that was adjacent the floor model TV. She sucked my dick and as if by magic the TV played a live broadcast of Monica and me. I could see the angles of her body as she sucked and stroked my dick. As she kneeled before me, my eyes wandered the room looking for the camcorder. She was taping us and playing it back in real time so I, I mean we could enjoy watching each other. It was shit like this that made me love her. No other female would ever do this type of shit. Watching her performance on the TV made my manhood grow stronger and harder.

Monica lay in the lounger as I gave her what she needed. My dick was penetrating her ass like it was pussy. It was just as wet and tight. I slapped that ass and watched it shake as she moaned with approval. She screamed harder, and I gave it to her harder. She would shake every time I took the head of my dick out and rammed it back into her. Monica took every inch of my massive beast. I knew I was blessed in the penis area. When I was a young boy, my dick was always a little bigger than the other boys. I could see that in the restrooms at school. Then when girls came along, they would say I was too big for them, or I was hurting them. Now, shiiid, even grown ass woman can't handle what I have. I measured myself once. 13.5 inches length when fully erect and the circumference the size of the circle your fingers make. So the fact that Monica could take me and I mean take me all no matter the position, told me she was worth keeping.

We fucked. And then we fucked again. We only broke our sweaty bodies apart to smoke a blunt and eat the spaghetti that Monic had prepared. It was delicious. It gave me the strength I needed to continue to hang with Monica's greedy sexual appetite. She was my demon and my angle. I wanted to be the man she needed, the man she craved. I was sure that she was feeling me too. I had known Monica for a while now and never have I heard about her cooking for a nigga. Not a one. Now her bedroom tricks, clapping her ass as she fucks me, all the tongue tricks she does while sucking my dick, all those might be new to me, but it's not something new for her. But cooking dinner, now that something new. I knew it was. Because Monica and I have talked about things that she would never do for a guy, and her cooking was on that list. So I knew that ol' girl was feeling me. She was feeling me the same way I was feeling her.

# "A Rose is Still a Rose"

**- Aretha Franklin**

**Yazz**

With tears in my eyes, I sat there, my hands folded. Anika and Monica sat there beside me. We were on the patio of the hotel Anika had called home for the past few weeks. What was supposed to be a going home celebration for Anika turned into some kind of intervention for me. I can't believe these bitches cornered me like this.

"Don't we have better things to be concentrating on than me?" I thought secretly to myself. Maybe it was time that I just let this cancer that has taken over my thoughts, my emotions, and my soul out of me. Maybe it was time that I cried for the girl I once was and the woman I have become. Maybe the release I've been longing for is right here in the arms of my sisters. The tears flowed steadily as I continued my journey.

"So, one night while Que and Jay left to take care of business. I was home alone. I just ordered take out from the Chinese restaurant a few blocks down the street. When the doorbell rang, I thought nothing of it. I must have been feeling real comfortable with my surrounds, or maybe it was the false sense of security that being with Jay provided me, but for the life of me I can't remember checking the peep hole or even grabbing the gun like I had done so many times before. I just didn't. I opened the door, and before I knew what the fuck happened, the door was kicked in. There was… I don't know… four or five guys with guns." I paused trying to catch my breath as tears rolled down my face. "Before I could do anything they grabbed me. They put a bag over my head and took me. "I bit my lower lip to keep from quivering. They took me. I don't know where. All I know is that it was about a twenty-minute ride. I could not tell what direction we were headed; I don't know the color of the car, I could not hear anything over my screaming." I added as I stared down at the cold concrete floor.

"I tried to remain calm, but I couldn't. How the fuck was I supposed to remain calm? I thought maybe it was revenge for them niggas that Jay and Que took care of that were following me. It could have been a thousand maybes, and it would not make a difference. They took me away from my comfort and …." I hesitated. "We pulled up to a building. I could hear people, but no one came to my rescue. I could hear them, and I know they heard my cries, but no one stopped them from taking me." The tears kept falling from my eyes. They tied me up to the rafters in the basement. I hung there like a punching bag as they ripped my clothes off of me while I pleaded and begged them to let me go. But there were no words spoken. With the bag still over my head, I was in darkness, alone. And all I could think about was all those people that Jay had killed. That this must be what it feels like to know you're going to die; to be powerless; to know that no matter what you say or do, your last breath was going to be taken from you. I hung there waiting, listening to my heartbeat. I had already stopped crying. I was just waiting for whatever was going to happen next." I spoke as I gazed up at Monica and Anika. Both of them had tears in their eyes for me. I wanted to tell them not to cry, but how could I. Hell, I needed to cry for her. I needed to give her a voice again because I knew I could never go back there. Back to a time where my naivety was more than surface deep. Where I choose a blind eye over the reality of this world we live in. I had straddled the fence long enough, and it was time to man up, so I choose to leave her behind in that space so that I could move on. So that I could breathe again; so that what happened to me would never happen again. I chose to become me; I choose the street because that was the only way I was going to survive this shit.

I continued, "I hung there lifeless for what felt like days. I could not feel my arms, nor my legs. By the time they had cut me down, my body was so numb, what they did to me next didn't even matter. One by one they raped me. With my hands and feet bound to the bedpost, they entered me. I lay there wanting to cry, but I would not give them the satisfaction. I lost count how many times they used me. After one would finish another nigga would climb on top of me. They did things to my body that I had reserved for only Jay. I tried to imagine being somewhere else, but I could not get there. I couldn't get there long enough to find my peace. Each one of them had a distinguishing scent. I hated that I had memorized them. Hated that the tone of their breathing hung over me, suffocating my senses, everything that covered my body. I hated that in all my years on this earth, the thought of anyone violating me had never crossed my mind. It was a thought that I had never entertained. And there I was repeatedly becoming a statistic, another lost soul and another victim of the streets."

I wanted to stop talking. I was like a leaking faucet; the words of my story pour out of me uncontrollably. There was no sense in turning me off now. The only way to fix what was ailing me was to just let all the poison out. I continued, "It seemed like days, as I lay there naked and afraid. My mind allowed me to doze off when I could escape my reality. I wondered what was next; I wanted to die, but I knew I had to fight. I didn't even know if I was worth fighting for anymore, I didn't even know if I had the strength to fight. I was through with the situation and came to realize that my story was more than this moment, and this would not define me.

"I was finally untied from the bedpost. I had assumed that they were going to kill me. I lay there on the bed tryna figure out what my next move would be; I could hear a lot of noise coming from outside the room I was in. I managed to get the bag off of my head and see my surroundings. It was dingy. The walls were a dirty beige, and the bed I was on was the only real furniture in the room. There were three milk crates I could only assume were used as chairs and newspaper plastered on the windows. I could hear the sounds getting louder and louder. I wasn't sure what to do, and there wasn't much time before someone came back into the room. There was nowhere to run, and the only place I could hide was in the small closet, nothing I could use as a weapon. The windows were nailed shut. I hide in the small closet as the sounds became more fierce and hard. I hide because it was the only option I had. I heard the door open, and someone walked through the room. I heard footsteps and tried my best not to cry or make any noise. I held my breath and had asked God to just end this nightmare. Either take me now while I still believe or let them just shot me. But I could not allow them to have what was left of me." I explained. I looked up just enough to see Anika crying and Monica watching me in silence. I could see the sorrow in her eyes. It was like she knew this feeling. Like she could identify with the hurt and pain, almost like she had walked that same mile in my shoes.

"I held onto that door knob for dear life. It slowly turned and grabbed it tighter ready to fight for what was left of me. They pulled, and I pulled harder. They pulled again, and I held on for dear life until I… I heard my name. I heard my name I cried. I cried because I thought he would never find me. I thought he thought that I had just left him. I cried because how could he love me after this? Like how could he want what was left of me? I let go of the door knob, and the door finally opened. It was Jay. He picked me up and held me in his arms. My body covered in the stench of other men's sweat. I was used and tortured, but he held me tight. He covered me with his tee shirt and jacket. He held me, and he cried. He walked me out of my prison and down a long hallway. I buried my head deep in his chest like a child. I could hear Que and Sleepy's voice. I lifted my head just to get a glimpse of what was happening. There they were, all of them. I could tell by the rhythm of their breathing and the tone of their pleading that it was them. All six of them kneeling begging for their lives. Put me down I yelled, and Jay hesitated but finally freed me from his grip. Without missing a step, I asked for the gun. I asked Jay to give me his gun, he obliged. I could hear him whisper, "you can't turn back from this. Once you pull that trigger, you can't undo it." I didn't care. I had too. I needed to end what they did to me. Jay waved for Que and Sleepy to hold off. Jay said that he would avenge me, which they would handle this, but it was too late. He could not stop what happened to me; he could not protect me. I had to protect myself. He could not undo what I just went through. No, I did not want his protection, I just wanted his gun, and I was sure I would survive what would happen next. I took the gun, pointed and pulled the trigger. The blow pack scared me, but I could not let that stop me from ending this. I pulled it again and again, again and again. I pulled the trigger and watched each of them fall. The blood splattered and poured out all over the floor. I wasn't scared. It did not even bother me. I pulled the trigger until there were no more bullets. I pulled the trigger until Jay took the gun out of my hand, I wanted to do more but what more could I do. They were dead; dead just like I had felt." I finished.

Anika and her big belly had wrapped her arms around me while Monica laid her head in my lap. There were tears as we sat in silence. They now knew what happen; I had finally laid to rest the person I once was. I gave her a voice once more and the satisfaction of knowing that we ended it. I knew that Anika and Monica cared; I knew that they would hold on to this secret. I knew that my sisters would hold me down; I knew that the tears we shared provided comfort and solace. We had done this many time before. The only one missing was Ayanna. I think at this moment; I cried because I knew she would have been here for me too. Oh, the shit we get ourselves into. This too shall pass, and when it does, I'll breathe again. Until then, I'll wear the armor the streets provided and I'll do my former self proud. Never again I thought. Never again.

# "Kissing You"

**-Total**

## Anika

I was happy to be heading home. Don't get me wrong; I loved that Que and I had time to talk and somewhat put our cards on the table. I know how he feels, and he knows what I need. My love for him could never change and it never will, but I needed more than empty promises. Hell, this baby and I needed consistency, and support, plus we deserved to be a family made up of a mother, father, and child. It was the way it had to be. I was just not sure if Que was truly made for that kind of life. On the other hand, Aaron could be, he had shown me nothing but love and support. Shit, I was wearing his engagement ring, yet, my heart would not listen to my mind.

It was a long ride back. Thank goodness Que had Monica and Yazz come up to make my drive back more relaxing, and after this morning's girl time, seems we had a lot to catch up on. It felt good to be able to cry and talk with my sisters. It had been too long and was overdue. We rode back to Buffalo in a black stretch limo. Que and I sat next to each other and Monica, and Yazz sat along the side. My feet were propped up, and Que was being the doting father and rubbing them. I shared with them the movements of the baby. Everyone taking turns rubbing my big ol' belly. We talked and joked, and it made the time go by fast.

We were about 30 minutes from Buffalo when all of a sudden, a sharp pain jabbed me in my lower back. It stopped me dead in my thoughts. I had to catch my breath. Everyone stared at me with puzzled looks.

"You good Ma?" Que asked

I shook my head yes trying to convince myself.

A few minutes went by, and again the pain hit me like the sting of a switch-hitting bare legs. I caught my breath and this time I grabbed hold of Que's hands as the pain intensified. The look on his face went from calm to serious stare.

"Anika, what's a wrong baby?" he asked

"I'm not sure. The pain" I uttered as I was hit by another dose of pain.

And before I knew it, there was a sudden urge gushing from between my legs. It was a steady stream of clear liquid flowing from me.

"Oh shit, oh shit" I muttered. "My water, it broke" I finished.

"WHAT!" Yazz screamed with excitement.

"IT'S BABYTIME!!" Monica yelled

Que had grabbed my hand and had kneeled beside me to check to see if what I had said was true.

"OH SHIT ANIKA! "What do we need to do?" he asked with a frantic look on his face.

"Calm down baby; I think we have some time. Someone needs to tell the driver we have a situation. I need to get to the hospital like now." I stated taking control of the conversation right before another round of pain engulfed me.

"SHIT!!!" I screamed as I tried to remember the breathing techniques that I had learned in Lamaze class.

"Hehehehehhe,     hahahaha,     hehehehe, hahahaha" I breathed in and out.

Que had grabbed some towel that he found by the champaign and ice bucket that was located behind Monica.

"Que, we need to get to the hospital quick. Her contractions are coming at a steady pace" Yazz commented.

"Just breathe," Monica said while looking around to see if she could find some more towels.

The Limo driver was going as fast as he could, Que had already spoken to him through the partition. We were about 15 minutes away now, and I wasn't sure I would make it. The contractions were starting to come pretty steady. Que had called the hospital to notify my doctor and the staff of our situation. He was told they would be waiting for us as soon as we arrived. Que needed to call back if there were any sudden changes or if I got the urge to push. Thank goodness for his burner phone, or else we all might be delivering this baby right here with no help. I was as calm as I could be. I was with the people who cared the most about me. Que had allowed Monica and Yazz to tend to me as he monitored my contractions and kept checking in between my legs to see if he saw he babies head crown. This was something the doctor on the phone told him to do, and the look on his face told me he was not very comfortable performing this task.

We finally made it into downtown Buffalo. My OBGYN was located at Children's Hospital. The driver got us over to Bryant Street within minutes. As we pulled into the emergency entrance, there was two nurses and a wheelchair waiting for me. Que helped me out of the Limo by picking me up and carrying me to the wheelchair. The nurses whisked me away through the double doors and quickly into a closed room. They checked to make sure that the fluid leaking out of me was, in fact, my amniotic fluid. Then they helped me get undressed, took a few vitals, connected me to some monitors and into a bed I went. They said I was about six centimeters dilated, but my contractions were progressing in their intensity. I was ready, sort of. Ready to finally meet my baby, but not ready to face my consequences. This baby was coming, and I better think about how this is going to play out. Me and Que or Me and Aaron, either way, one person would win the prize; I just hope that I'm on the winning side of things.

# "No One Else Comes Close"

- Joe

## Aaron

I jumped in the car as soon as I got the call. I'm on my way baby. Daddy is on his way. I Could never miss the birth of my child. I was so happy the hospital called me. Anika and I had her emergency contact information updated a few months back during one of her doctor appointments. We thought it would be best if the doctor or hospital needed to get in contact with me if something happened to Anika or the baby. I just hoped Anika and the baby are ok. The nurse did not say much other than Anika had been checked into the hospital and that she was dilated 6 centimeters with steady contractions. It was the moment I had been waiting for. My baby was having my baby. Lord knows I loved Anika; she was perfect for me. From the way she made me feel, her smile, and the way she supported me.  I promise from here on out that I will get my shit together. All this extra side chick and sissy shit had to stop. It was going to be about Anika and our baby. I would make her proud of me; I had too. I just had to control my urges; I need to leave all that shit behind me before I lose it all.

I was almost there. The hospital was 10 minutes away. I prayed she was doing good. I could not wait to see her. I knew even in labor, Anika would still be the most beautiful woman in the room. I turned right onto Elmwood Avenue from West Ferry; I was almost there. And with any luck, I won't miss a thing. I couldn't help but think about Anika, the baby, and soon we would be a family. I smiled at the thought. Anika wanted to wait until after the baby was born before we got married. I think she just didn't want to walk down the aisle pregnant. I told her it would not matter what she was wearing; she would always be the most beautiful woman in the world to me. She smiled and still insisted on waiting, which was cool. It gave me a chance to finish up my training sessions, among other things.

I did not have time to think about my extracurricular activities. Just thinking of who might be out there trying to blackmail me, or end my career made me sick. I was getting mad at the thought of Anika finding out about my secret. This would kill her, and I was not about to let anything come between her and me. This included Que. Knowing that Yazz was back meant that he was not too far off. I'm sure he'll want to come back for Anika, but with any luck, Anika and I will be happily married by then. Once the baby is born, Que wouldn't stand a chance coming between us. I know how serious Anika takes having a family. She made it very clear to me how she wanted to raise the baby, and being a single parent or divorcing was not an option — her words not mine. Besides, I was going to ask her to marry me anyway; the baby was just a bonus.

I had pulled into the adjacent parking lot. I walked across the street and into the emergency room. It was game time; I was ready to quarterback the delivery of my first child. With camcorder in hand, I was ready to welcome my child into this world and ready to be a father. All that other bullshit did not matter, I would figure this out somehow, but today was all about Anika and the baby. Daddy was here, and It was time for me to find Anika so we can start the show.

# "Beauty"

**- Dru Hill**

**Que**

I had finished filling out the paperwork that the lady at the check-in desk asked me to complete. I was amazed at how much I knew about Anika. There wasn't one question that I could not answer. From blood type to last doctor visit, I knew all that shit. Why wouldn't I? Even when I was in Michigan, I had kept tabs on her and the baby. I know her shoe, bra and pants size. I know everything from her favorite color, fashion designer, and perfume. I had taken notes on Anika my whole life, ever since we were kids. She likes Butter Pecan and Crazy Vanilla Hershey's ice cream. Anika eats french fries with malt vinegar and extra salt. And her favorite pop was Tahitian Treat and Peach Nehi. Make no mistake; I also knew all the things this woman did not like. I made sure not to forgot that list. When it came to loving Anika, she made it so easy. She was my around the way girl, my queen; she could be hood and a debutante all at once. She made knowing all this easy, and why wouldn't I want to know everything about the women I love that's about to have my seed?

I could now see Anika. The Nurse took me back to her room. Anika was in active labor so they had, moved her up to the labor and delivery floor. I was instructed to go to room 411. I had arranged for Anika to have a private room. While checking her in, I had mentioned to the nurse that I would be paying for the labor and delivery. I want Anika to be as comfortable as possible. I asked about the sizes of the rooms, and what our options were, this was something I had also looked into a while in Michigan. I took the elevator up to the fourth floor and headed to her room. I knocked and walked in. I could hear Yazz and Monica talking. I turned the privacy curtain and to see both of them comforting her. I walked over and kissed her forehead; she looked beautiful. Anika was lying in bed with her feet birched. I looked at Yazz and Monica, and without a word, they knew what I was asking. They excused themselves from the room and went to wait in the family waiting room. I just wanted some time with the woman I loved before we welcomed our baby into this world.

I lay in the bed next to her, breathing in her scent. I held on to her and rubbed her hair. I coached her through her contractions and even fed her ice chips. I helped her walk the room, and we even did some squats and bounces to help with the pain. The nurse kept coming in the room to check on Anika; her labor was advancing. She now measured eight centimeters, and the contractions were starting to increase in intensity. It was almost time. I could tell it was taking a toll on Anika. I was rubbing her back and trying to keep her as relaxed as I could. My heart was full of excitement and worry. I hated seeing her like this. The pain seemed unbearable, yet, I knew that this was the beginning of living my life with purpose. From here on out, it was not just about me, but Anika and my seed. I would not let them down.

# "Money Ain't a Thang"

**- Jermaine Dupri ft. Jay Z**

**Yazz**

I was sitting in the waiting room with Monica. I'm hella happy for my girl, but there was just one thing that that we needed to take care of. I had waited long enough, it was either now or never. I was just waiting for Jay and Mario to show up so that I could share with them what I've been up to. I figured they would know best how to handle this situation. I called Jay on the burner. He and Mario were heading to the hospital and were less than 5 minutes away. Monica was busy looking at the old issue of Ebony Magazine that was left on the coffee table of the waiting room. I looked at the door to the waiting room opened; It was a carrier. We made eye contact as he made his way over to me. He handed me the envelope and the note attached. I gave him a stack for delivering the package with urgency. He left just as quickly as he appeared. I knew the contents of the package; there was no need to look inside. I just wanted to make sure Jay, Mario, and Monica were on board with my game plan. I was out to make sure no one I cared about getting hurt. There was too much at stake. Besides, what happens in the dark always come to light. I just happened to be the match that strikes the candle first.

The next time the door to the waiting room opened, it was Jay and Mario. I walked over to greet Jay with a kiss. He asked was Que was at. I told him that he was in the room with Anika. I brought him up to speed on Anika and the baby. I could tell he was excited too; he was about to be an uncle. Maybe one day this could be Jay and me. But not right now, we still had some things to work out and talk about before I bring a baby into the mix. What I did notice while Jay and I were talking were Mario and Monica. Both me and Jay took a double look. There was something going on between those two. I'm sure Monica will fill me in later. Right now, we had a bigger issue to handle.

I grabbed the manila legal size envelope the carrier brought to me. I showed the contents to Jay.

"YO! WHAT THE FUCK?" he yelled out in disbelief.

"I know right. This shit is crazy" I replied as he called Mario over to the corner we were standing in. Mario broke free from his conversation with Monica and came over to see what all the excitement was about.

"YO KID! THAT'S SOME SHIT RIGHT THERE!" Mario said bussing out in laughter. "Yo MO come look at this shit." he continued.

Monica came over to take a look and immediately gasped for air. "Is that who I think it is?" she questioned holding the pictures closer for a better look.

"There's more" I added. "It seems that someone's been very busy and I have proof."

I began to fill everyone in on my suspicions. I had heard from a few people about Aaron and his extracurricular bullshit. It started just before we left for Michigan. The last time I was at the hair salon, one of the stylist was talking about her new Boo. She was giving too much detail and even had a picture as proof. I figured that Anika and Aaron's relationship was still young and I wasn't sure how exclusive they were, so I tucked it away until I could get more information. But then we left. The same thing happened in Detroit. A girl in the salon was bragging about her man in Buffalo, and how he played for the Buffalo Bills. She met him while in Florida. Everything she said from description to the way he operated screamed Aaron. So I decided to hire a private detective to find out just what Aaron was up to. To my surprise, I found out more than I initially thought.

"So I spent the money to find out just what he was up to. I had Aaron followed for a few months, and the information was solid. This nigga got bitches in every state, town, and in between. He hasn't been faithful to Anika at all. From day one, he has been tryna play my girl. Then to top it off, this nigga swings both ways. Talk about a game changer. This nigga has been given up the dick to everyone." The three of them stood there in disbelief at what they had just heard, but the pictures were the proof. "So I had Aaron followed. I even set him up a few times and that nigga failed each one of the tests I set up, it was too easy. And the very last test, the picture you just saw, the guy he was with was all for helping to set him up. He left the door unlocked so that the private detective could get a really good picture of him in the act. The only thing is I did not want to stress Anika out with this information. With everything that was happening, I did not want to add to her pain. However, I think we can all agree that the charade is up. I think that Que needs to know. Do yall agree?" I asked.

"Most def. Que needs to know" Mario spoke up nodding his head.

"Let me get him, what room is he in?" Jay asked heading to room 411. Monica sat there reviewing all photos that detailed the months of lies Aaron had, all the deceit that he had done, all along planning to be married to Anika. Not to mention fathering her baby. It was time this nigga got what was coming to him. All that money and Aaron couldn't buy privacy. He put his business in the streets fuckin' with all these tricks and bitches, and for what? I'll tell you about what, for nothing. Because when I'm done with him, there won't be anything left of him.

# "Humpin' Around"

### - Bobby Brown

## Aaron

"Excuse me, Ma'am, can you tell me which floor is the labor and delivery? I got a call that my fiancée is in active labor; I just need to find her." I questioned as my heart raced at the thought of her being by herself. The older gray haired lady at the desk smiled warmly at me. She asked what was the name of my fiancée? I told her "Anika Deveaux." She immediately wrote down the room number on a piece of paper, handed it to me, and pointed to the elevators to the right of her. With her instructions fresh in my mind I did just as she had instructed. I was on my way to my baby girl and our baby. I pushed the fourth-floor button and the doors closed.

When the doors opened, I walked right over to the information desk. The lady was on the phone. I tried being as patient as I could, but under the circumstances, it was hard just to wait; this was an emergency. I tried interrupting the lady, but she kept holding up her fucking finger to imply that she would be right with me. As I stood there waiting, I had a strong feeling that I was being watched. I surveyed the room and what do you know, Anika's homegirls were already here. Didn't know why that did not surprise me… they were always fucking around. This was something I would put a stop to once we were married. I did not want these nosy ass bitches messing up my relationship. I smiled as I dare go over to the to find out how I could get back to Anika's room. But the unwelcoming looks on their faces told me I would be better off waiting for the lady at the help desk.

Finally, the lady was done with her phone call. "Hi ma'am, my fiancée is in room 411, and I need to get back there. Can you help me?" I asked with urgency. The look on her face showed concern and made me feel like something may have gone wrong, possibly with Anika or the baby, maybe even both. "Ma'am, can you help?" I questioned.

"Well, it seems that Ms. Deveaux already has a visitor in the room with her right now, you will have to wait. I'll let you know when you can go back," she answered looking over in the direction of Monica and Yazz. This is some bullshit, I thought. Who the fuck was back there with her. I immediately thought of her mother. With this being the first grandchild, of course, her mother would be here. It would also explain why Tweedle Dee and Tweedle Dumb are not back there with her.

I walked over to Yazz and asked, if they had been able to see Anika and if she was ok. Without any reason, Yazz swung off and punched the shit out of me. Everyone in the waiting room instantly looked in our direction. It caught me off guard. Weirdly I like,d it. After all the bitch was fine, and any other day I might have taken this as an invitation for something else, so the bitch was lucky we had and audience or I might have taken her right here. But I know how to handle her. Pretty soon the trio would have one less member because there was no way in hell my baby and Anika was going to be hanging out with these hoes. Monica sat there laughing.

"Nigga she punched the shit out of him" Monica chimed in with her stanky ass.

"What the fuck was that for Yazz?" I said wiping the blood out the corner of my mouth.

"You'll find out soon enough" she replied.

"What the hell is that supposed to mean?" I questioned.

"Nigga, I'm surprised she didn't shoot yo' ass. You better calm the fuck down before…" Monica was interrupted by the lady at the desk.

"Is there a problem? Is everything ok over there?" She questioned.

"We're good" I replied.

"Fuck both of yall" I stated in a more mellow voice.

I did not come here for this shit. I wanna see Anika. I walked over to the other side of the room and waited. My impatience or my stinging jaw got the best of me because, after about 10 minutes of waiting, the doors to the rooms opened from an orderly exiting the area and before the doors could close I quietly entered. Now to find room 411.

# "Victory"

## - Puff Daddy and the Family

**Que**

"Is this Nigga fo' real? Yo, you got a lot of nerve showing your face up in here." I yelled as I charged after his gay ass. Before I knew it, my hands were wrapped around his neck as I hemmed Aaron up against the wall to the delivery room. The anger I was feeling right now overpowered the calm I was feeling just minutes prior. I could hear Anika screaming for me to stop. I could not hold back, and there was no pleading that would stop me him ending this punk muthafuckas life.

**Aaron**

I had opened the door, and to my surprise, Anika was not with her mother. Before I could even think, Que had charged after me. With every punch and swing, he laid into me, all I could think about was what the fuck was happening. Why was this nigga going so hard? Was he mad that I got Anika pregnant? That she told him that we were getting married? Mad that he left a good thing behind? Mad that she chose me instead of him? All the punches in the world won't change the fact that I won. That I got the girl and his thug ass lost. Hatin' ass nigga.

His home boy finally was able to get him off me. I could see Anika crying in the background. This shit was stressing her out. Que didn't know it, but he had a lawsuit coming. I was going to take the girl and his cash. Stupid ass nigga.

"Welcome home Nigga" I gloated as I rubbed the blood off the corner of my mouth with a paper towel. "You made it home just in time to see Anika give birth to my baby" I added with a smirk on my face.

## Que

"Yo son, you don't honestly think that this baby is yours? Nigga that baby is mined. She was pregnant before I left; I remember the night I planted that seed. But that's cute; I didn't take you for the daddy type. Ain't you more like the skirt wearing type? Didn't think your boys swam in shit that could get someone pregnant" I said looking his gay ass up and down. "Nigga what you need to do is leave before I bust a cap off in yo ass" I continued as Jay stood in between us. I could hear Anika cries for me to stop, but she had no idea. She had no clue who the hell this muthafucka was. I stood there allowing Jay to hold me back. It was taking everything in me not to just handle Aaron right here and now. "TELL THIS MUTHAFUCKA ANIKA!" I yelled. "Tell Mr. Cornerback who the fuck I am. Tell him once and for all who I am and why." I spoke stern looking only at him, eye to eye, daring him to make a fuckin' move.

Anika sat there quiet. He looked at her and then back at me. "ANIKA! TELL HIM NOW, AND LET'S PUT THIS SHIT TO REST! I yelled out.

"Que this is not how I wanted to do this" Anika pleaded.

"NOW" I reiterated. I could hear her cries and pleads, but they meant nothing to me right now. This triflin' ass nigga; she had no idea. The anger inside of me inched closer and closer to me grabbing my .09 and blastin' his ass.

## Aaron

"Stop yelling at my fiancée! You can't make her say anything, especially if it's not true. Who the fuck you think you are? This ain't them streets; you don't run shit up in here" I spoke up. I could tell that all this commotion was not good for Anika and the baby. She was grabbing at her belly as she was trying to plead with this asshole. The blood from my lip continued to roll down, and I continued to wipe it away. "You should have never left her. If you cared so much about her you should have stayed, better yet, you should have taken her with you. You left her. You didn't love her then, and you don't love her more than I do" I added. She's having my baby and will be my wife. Playa', I'm sure you can find another bitch to play your games with, but Anika is all the woman I need and more. She's mines now." I said flexing as my face harden.

**Que**

"Nigga is this what you think?" I said pushing Jay out of my way. I charged after Aaron and quickly found him in my grip again. "Nigga I told you. Do remember our conversation? Huh? Do you remember what I told you? I warned you. I told you to take care of her, do you remember that? I told you, you had better take care of her or else. I warned you. And now you went pay" I finished. My hand connected to his face once more. As he fell to the floor of the delivery room, I proceeded to stomp the shit out of him. My boot caught his face, head, and chest. I could hear Anika crying, but this time it was different. She had gone from pleas to a cry of pain. It was enough to catch my attention. I immediately stopped the step show I was performing on Aaron and went to her side.

"Baby are you ok?" I asked with sincerity taking her hand.

"QUE!" she screamed out, taking a long breath.

"Breath Anika. Just breathe baby" I encouraged.

It was a contraction, and it was stronger than the last one. The whole interaction was enough for Aaron to muster up enough strength to get his weak ass off the floor and standing again. The look on his face was... it almost looked like he wanted to do something to me.

**Aaron**

"Anika" I called out. "Anika, tell him. Tell him I'm the father?" I begged. "Get away from my fiancée and my baby" I whispered trying to catch my breath.  My eyes would barely open, they were starting to swell from Que using my face as a stepping stone, but I could see enough to know that Anika found comfort in Que. I saw enough to know that this nigga was not going to go quietly and leave Anika alone. I stood there watching, as the nurse and doctor came into the room. We must have been making a lot of noise as the security guard stood at the doorway looking to escort someone out the room. Well, it won't be me. I'm staying right here. Right next to my fiancée and our baby. "Security, security, can you please escort this boy out of this room. He is stressing out my fiancée; this can't be god for the baby." I commanded.

"We're going to need both of you to leave" the uniformed male figure spoke.

"Both of us? I questioned. "He attacked me. Just look at me" I demanded. "I'm not going anywhere. My fiancée is having my baby; I'm supposed to be here, this asshole is the one that needs to leave. He's not welcomed here." I added.

## Que

"The baby is mined. As far as leaving, you're the only one that's about to get out. You can leave peacefully, and I'll deal with you later, or you can leave by force, either way, you about to get the fuck out of the way and out of my sight" I swore. "You can stand there looking like the victim if you want with your gay ass, but what you ain't gone do is play me like one of those sissy ass niggas you been wit'. Yeah, that's right, you thought your secret was safe. Naw nigga, ain't shit you do safe or a secret. You fucked with the wrong girl. It wasn't any way in hell that I was going to let you play Anika like that, and now you wanna play daddy nigga? Bitch, you better step the fuck back before you catch a bullet to the dome; I'll end you and your career with one smooth shot. Now, what Nigga!? Say something else with your faggot ass" I spoke as I saw the look in his eyes sober him up to the reality of his indiscretions.

## Anika

"What are you talking about Que?" I questioned in between my contractions. The look on Aaron's face reminded me of a child that had been caught with his hands in the cookie jar before dinner, and Que was the parent waiting to administer punishment. Harsh punishment. The room was silent. Even the security guard had stopped in his tracks after Que spoke his thoughts. There they stood, staring at each other, the two men I had loved. One I was in love with and one I loved. "WHAT IS GOING ON!?" I yelled as another round of Contractions started. "QUE... AARON... NOW!" I managed to scream as I breathed through the contraction and the urge to push. The nurse rushed to my side. She began to check my vitals and asked to check my progress. She confirmed that I was now 8 centimeters dilated. I could tell that something had changed as the intensity of the contractions worsened. "HEE, HEE, HAW, HAW, OOHHHHH" I let out as I breathed through the contraction and tried to focus on the baby.

"OOOHHHH, HEE, HEEE, HAA, HAA!" I grunted trying to relax and breathe.

## Aaron

It was this nigga. This nigga set me up. I should have known it was him. Who else would go to such lengths to destroy what Anika and I have? I could feel the fire in me building up. All the shit this nigga into, and he wanna come for me? He wanna take everything that matters to me away, threaten my career, my girl and our baby? I would kill him first. "Anika, listen, baby, I need to tell you something. I wanted to tell you first, but not like this. I… I…

## Que

I… I… What nigga? You wanna tell Anika now. Wanna you tell her all about your little rendezvous while you were away? Wanna you confess now? Wanna you tell her this shit now? I oughta' kill you right now!" I interrupted Aaron while reaching for my gun.

## Aaron

"Anika it's not what you think. I would never do anything to hurt you, baby. You know how much I love you. I just wasn't thinking." I pleaded, looking past Que to see the sadness on Anika's face. "Anika, I love you so much. You're everything I need and more. And the baby, we can move past this and be a family. I know I can make you happy. Anika… Anika baby… I'm so sorry… Baby, I'll never…"

## Que

"You'll never what?" I questioned. "Fuck other bitches or fuck other niggas? Which one? Because according to the pictures, you've been a dirty boy." I said throwing the pictures that Yazz had given me at him. The pictures glided to the floor surrounding him like a pool of water. He stood there in silence, looking at me, them, then Anika. Looking for sympathy, but I ain't that nigga, and the only thing I want to give right now is a bullet with his name on it.

**Anika**

"Aaron, is this true? I asked not wanting to hear the answer. I could tell by the look on his face that every word Que spoke was the truth. I choked as I could not figure out if I wanted to cry or let the contraction overtake me, so I gave into both. "HOW COULD YOU!? OTHER WOMEN!?" I screamed through the contraction as the nurse coached me.

She had asked the security guard to escort the men out of the room once again. The security guard took one look at Que's face and knew not to make a move or say a word, so he stood there witnessing the drama. "Aaron, you're gay... I don't understand. You've been with men, how could you...? love me and do this...? I don't understand." I cried through the contraction.

**Aaron**

"Anika it's not what you think baby. I'm not gay, I just … I mean… I'm so sorry." I pleaded. "I love you, that's all that matters. I'll never hurt you again… Baby, I'm so sorry." I cried out loud trying to convince Anika that what we have is real, but the pictures of me with various women and men littered the floor around me. I could see the faces,

I knew the names, places, and I remember the sex. They had been watching me for a while. I wished I could take it all back. I wished that I had the self-control to tame my desires, I wished that I had never seen the look on Anika's face. My heart hurt worse then than any physical pain that had been directed towards me in the previous moments. "Anika, I love you and the baby. I need you. I can't live without you" I made my pleas heard one last Time. "He can't love you as I can, he can't give you the life you want. He can't do the things I can for you; give you what you need and deserve" I prayed to confess my love, feeling like it was falling on deaf ears.

## Que

"Anika tell this fool who the father of your child is" I insisted. "Put this muthafucka out his misery now I begged before my bullet do it for you" I added as I stood there with my gun in hand. Anika sat up in the hospital bed ready for the next contraction. The nurse had checked her once more and had called for the doctors to come in. It was time. Time for the baby to arrive and time to put an end to this bullshit. Aaron stood waiting; I stood to wait; there was only one thing left. Anika, feeling another contraction coming on with tears in her eyes spoke.

## Anika

"Que is the father of my baby," I spoke clear and deliberately, so there was no misunderstanding in my words. "Que is the father" I spoke again as the tears rolled down my face, looking at Aaron. It was the final answer that said it all. It was the truth. It was the only thing that had made since to me for the past 9 months; it was the only thing that I had lived for. It was the love I had been looking for and the family I had wanted. It was something I could not deny any further. My baby was Que's. And now everyone would know, Aaron included. And with that, it was time to push. Que had rushed to my side, all the while looking at Aaron. I knew this was not the end of the two of them. Que never left business unfinished, and Aaron was business that he needed to set straight. I could see Aaron picking up the photos off the hospital floor. Other than my moans and grunts the room was silent. Jay watched as Aaron gathered up the photos and then both of them were escorted out of the room by the security guard. It was the beginning and the end. With Que by my side and the direction of the doctor and nurses, I pushed. I pushed through the pain I had caused; the lies I told; the betrayal of Aaron, and the heartache from Que. I breathed and bared down and pushed and pushed and let go of all that I had been through and welcomed my baby into the world.

# "I Don't Ever Wanna See You Again"

### - Uncle Sam.

## Anika

I could not be happier. I had been blessed with two healthy baby boys. I don't know how all this time the doctors could not tell I was having twins. It's not uncommon for one of the babies to hide and go undetected on the ultrasound. I had been in the hospital for almost a week. I had lost a large amount of blood, and the doctors thought I was hemorrhaging after giving birth, so they kept me to monitor my blood levels and make sure that there were no other issues. The best part was I got to be with my babies. Que had spent every day and night with me. My mother had been up here to visit and a host of family members. The gifts from members of the FAM and other associates poured in. We had two of everything. There were so many gifts that the hospital staff had to place me in another room. Everyday Que had someone come to the hospital to pack up the gifts and take them to the new house. I felt like a spoiled princess. Monica and Yazz had been up here visiting every day. They had already made plans to spoil the boys. I knew with those two looking after my sons they would be in good hands. And rightfully so after all they both would be the god-mothers.

I was expecting Que any moment. I had the nurse bring the boys to me. They had been in the nursery resting. I had learned very quickly that when they slept, I had to sleep also. But it was feeding time, and with two babies, I had to make sure that I had a tight schedule and that I stuck to it. I was in the middle of feeding the twins when there was a knock at the door. I assumed it was either Que, Monica or Yazz. The door opened, and it was Aaron. There was silence. It was awkward. The last time we saw each other, there were lies and confessions and heartache and pain. Neither one of us deserved what we did to each other, but I did not think that we would ever be in a position to see each other again.

"They are beautiful," Aaron said grinning. "Just like their mother" he added.

"Thank you" I replied as I continued breastfeeding. There was more silence. All I kept thinking was if Que were to walk in and see Aaron there was no telling what he would do next. "Aaron, what are you doing here?" I asked with a puzzled look on my face.

There was silence. He just stood there looking at the babies and me. "Aaron, Que will be back any moment, I just can't. I don't want a repeat of the last time you both were here. Why are you here?" Aaron looked at me the way he had done so many times. I knew that he loved me, but we could never be together. Not after the lies and the pain we caused each other.

"I just wanted to tell you how sorry I am. I'm sorry for everything that I put you through." Aaron whispered.

"You don't owe me anything, Aaron. We both did some things that we can never take back." I stated

"Yeah you're right, but I need you to know I never meant to hurt you. I do care about you. I do love you; it's just..." Aaron spoke hesitating.

"Aaron, you don't have to explain anything to me. You don't owe me anything. Here," I said reaching in the side draw to the hospital side table. I gave him the engagement ring. The ring I had worn so proudly before now was just a symbol of deceit and betrayal. "Take this Aaron," I said looking him in the eyes. "Aaron, we should have never been together. I think we were just filling the empty void of something that we both were missing. You need to figure out what you are, and you know what I mean. You put me and the health of my babies in jeopardy. How could you? How could you not protect yourself and me? You need to have an honest conversation with yourself. You better figure your shit out soon, before someone else decides for you." I continued.

"Anika, I'm not gay, I mean I… I just don't… I …"

"Aaron, it doesn't matter to me. You're the one who needs to figure that out."

"But I love you; I thought we, you could have made me the man I'm meant to be. I just wanted to be that for you and your babies. Hell, I knew the baby wasn't mined. I didn't care. I just wanted to be with you." Aaron confessed.

"Aaron, there could never be an us. And as long as Que was the father you could never take his place. I'm so sorry that I put you in that space. It would never have worked out." I said trying to master breastfeeding and burping at the same time.

Aaron stood there looking down at me. He watched wishfully. Full of hope for a what if that was no longer an option for him and me.

"Aaron, you need to leave," I stated.

He just stood there. His eyes are full of sadness and confusion.

"Aaron" I called out. He came to and agreed. He took one last look and smiled that smile I once loved and admired. He turned and walked out of the room without a goodbye. Maybe saying goodbye was too final for him to bare. His surprise visit was the unwelcomed closure I needed. It was the end to my beginning and a new chapter in my life. One I would openly embrace with the man I loved and the family I always wanted.

# "I Don't Wanna Be A Playa No More"

### - Big Pun ft. Joe

## Mario

The crew and I got Anika and Que moved into their new home out in Blasdell, NY. It was way out of the way, very secluded and away from the rough streets of Buffalo. But most importantly, it was a chance to separate the business from the life Que and Anika were finally trying to create. I mean damn, I had not known two people so destined to be together would have to fight so hard to make it happen. We all knew at some point Anika, and Que would be together, it just seemed like the timing was always off. But this time they seemed to get it together. I'm sure the birth of the twins helped out a lot. Whatever it takes, I'm just glad that Que finally got his woman, and now it was time for me to do the same.

I headed back to the city. The whole ride I was thinking about Monica. That girl brought a smile to my face and a stiff dick to my pants. She had me feignin' not just for what was between her legs, but her attitude, that sexy ass walk, and the way she could switch it up and be street and classy at the drop of a hat. She was the one, and I could not fight it anymore. Plus, I knew I had her heart. Without labeling each other, we were the closest thing to a couple. We spent every day and free hours together; I damn near stayed at her place. Monica knew the game and respected the business. She was as much a part of the FAM as I was. I trusted her with my life, and I would take that bullet for her just like I would Que and Jay. With everyone else coupled up, it was time I made it official with Monica. Let all them other niggas that be sniffing around know that she was off limits. Let the streets know that I claimed and marked my territory. Yeah, I was ready, I was going to hang up that hat and trade my playa' card in for Monica.

I pulled up to Monica's crib. She was sitting on the porch puffin on a blunt. She had on a red tube top and a pair of cut of jean shorts that showed all of her thick thighs that I usually saw wrapped around my neck as I gave it to her good. She stood up and not only could you see her thighs, but the jean shorts accentuated her ass and barely covered it. Her name necklace hung between her cleavage and her curly hair swayed in the wind as a soft breeze graced her midriff. She was my drug; I could sniff her every day and get high. She walked to the end of the porch with nothing on her feet and waited for me to approach with a smile on her face. I was a sucka' at that moment. A sucka' for love and a thug for the streets. What has this bitch done to me?

I should have run when I had the chance. Monica was nothing but trouble, yet I was drawn to her like a magnet. Her pull on me was hypnotizing. Her perfume was mesmerizing as I stood there cuffing her ass as we hugged for the whole neighborhood to see. I picked her up as she wrapped those legs around my waist and I carried her over to the hood of my car and placed that phat ass down on my ride. She sat there picturesque like we were getting ready to do a video and she was the vixen. Monica's eyes were beautiful. The perfect shade of brown. I turned the music up in the car and allowed the amplifiers to pound out bass from the songs that played. Monica began to move her body to the beat and put on a personal show for me that was worthy of the center stage at the strip clubs. This is why I loved her and had to make her mines. Shit like this, without even thinking she did things that had a nigga wanting to bust. The way she moved drove me crazy and had me excited for whatever would come next.

I walked over to her as she stopped her performance. She was sitting with her legs spread open and I walked right in between them. She scooted up towards me until our bodies met. I took a puff of her blunt and passed it back. With nothing but the music playing we rocked to the beat and puffed on the blunt. No words were spoken, just the unwritten code that brought us together and that magnetic force that kept us in sync. That was until Monica noticed something in my pocket. She reached in my front pocket and pulled out my surprise. I knew I had gotten it right by the look on her face. The smile was worth a million words and more valuable than all the stash I could sell. I raised my eyebrows and backed away from her, and asked: "So Ma, don't you think we should take this relationship to the next level?"

I stood there waiting, knowing that the answer was already yes, but I needed to hear her say it. She had placed the ring on her finger and was already checking the carat size and sparkle.

"Ma, you gone leave a nigga waiting?" I questioned.

Monica few off the hood of the car and ran straight into my arms.

"YES, NIGGA, YES!" she screamed and sealed it with a kiss. "YES!" she let out one last cry and began doing the happy girl dance. I watched her, that red tube top and them short shorts. All that was going to be mines, all mines. I was leaning against the car watching her. I wasn't nervous, had no doubts. I know that it would not be easy, but it would be worth it. Besides, I had already seen enough drama to know if you don't act with urgency, something or someone else would. I ain't got time for that kind of bullshit. The life I lead doesn't guarantee me too many tomorrows, so I'm living for today. And Monica was a part of me that would make today worthwhile, and hopefully, we could grow to see tomorrow together.

Monica had calmed down just enough to notice me watching her. The look in her eyes told me she was ready to show me her gratitude. She had made her way over to me and managed to cuff my dick in her hands. It was heavy and ready to break free. The way she bites her bottom lip and the devious look on her face told me she was going to break him out, and without hesitation, she greeted me with the thanks I deserved. In her driveway, between two houses, as the sun set, and the breeze crossed my exposed dick, Monica bowed down and sucked me like never before. I leaned against the car and gave my wife to be everything I had, and she graciously accepted a mouthful of thanks. Between two houses in her driveway, Monica had solidified why she was the one for me, and she drank it all, in that red tube top and them damn short shorts. Yeah, this is what I wanted, and she wanted me too.

# "Elevators"

**-Outkast**

**Jay**

I woke up to the smell of bacon and everything good on a Sunday morning. I reached for Yazz to notice she was not laying beside me. That could only mean one thing; my baby was in the kitchen cooking. Yazz made it a point to always cook on Sundays. It was one of the few days and times during the week that we had time just to chill. Sundays were for family and today we were heading over to Que's and Anika's to visit my Godsons and eat dinner. It would be us, Monica and Mario. Just the immediate crew. It was normal we all craved in the life we lived. Doing shit everyday people did. No looking over your shoulder, watching what the next nigga was doing, counting money, checking on the territory, handling business, just hanging out with family no extra shit needed. I had grabbed my robe and headed downstairs to the kitchen. Yazz had it smelling good. The aroma of bacon, hot syrup and biscuits filled the whole house. It was surprising after surprise 'cause Yazz was owning the kitchen wearing nothing but a lace apron and some feather high heels. She was looking just as good as the house smelled and I was hungry as hell for both her and the food.

I watched in silence as Yazz made her way around the kitchen oblivious to my standing there. It told me that she felt safe, which was a long way from the event in Michigan. Everything had been better lately. She told me that she had shared with Anika and Monica what had happened to her. Just thinking about it makes me so angry inside. What they did to Yazz, what she went through, I blame me. I would take the rest of my life making it up to her. I swear on my life I would not let anything else happen to her ever again and I know she knows that now. I would never put her in harm's way again, but let Yazz tell it, she can protect herself now, with all the boxing and karate classes she has taken. I feel sorry for the next nigga that walks up on her. Not to mention the fact that she has perfect aim. She was my Bonnie, and as her Clyde, I needed to give her the space she needed to get better. But I wasn't expecting Bonnie 2.0 in return. Yazz was harder and tougher and no longer timid or scared of anything. ANYTHING! That in itself meant I needed to protect her even more, and maybe even from herself.

Yazz finally let go of the music that had entranced her and notice me admiring her curves and moves in the kitchen. The white and baby pink thong and the matching apron looked just as good as those hot buttered biscuits that sat on top of the stove. She stood there fingering me to come closer; it was all the invitation I needed. I was hungry, and there was nothing that yelled come and eat faster than Yazz, that thong, and the lace apron. I walked over to her as she summoned and without asking picked her up and placed her on the island countertop. She smiled as I laid her back on the cold granite, slid the thong to the side and began to eat my breakfast. There was nothing sweeter than the juice that poured out of Yazz as she wiggled and moaned to my tongue as it licked her lips and fingered her ass and pussy at the same time.

I ate like I had been starved and was malnourished. I took my time and made sure not to rush just like my momma had taught me. I licked, and my tongued played her clitoris like a drum and then soft like the strings of a violin. She tried to get away from the intensity of my music, but I pulled her back into my grip and enjoyed watching her squirm and moan. I ate and drank to my contentment, and there was nothing she could do. Yazz lay there and surrendered to me; it was something I thought I would never get back. It was a feeling that took me and her months to get back to, and I wanted her to know that no matter what I needed her, that she could trust me, and I could love her despite what happened. I knew by her response to my tongue and fingers that she knew. There were no more fights between us. We were no longer enemies on the same team, but we were one, just a better version.

She gave herself to me as she fucked me back. I had picked her up and allowed her to ride my face as I stuck my tongue deep into her pussy and my fingers into her ass. I gripped her ass as she held my head and I rocked her back and forth as her legs wrapped around my neck. She screamed out in pleasure as we rocked harder and harder as my tongue fucked her and fingers entered in and out of her. I licked and licked as she rode my fingers like a thick dick. She was wet, and my carnal hunger grew even more. I growled as she moaned. We were like two wild beasts fucking without a cause. The pure ecstasy and animal attraction would not allow us to stop. I wanted all of her, and she needs to release. She moaned, and

I licked. She bucked, and I held her even tighter into me. I twisted my tongue, massaged her lips and clit.

I hit spots that she did not know even existed, as hot liquid cascaded down from her and into my mouth and all over my face. She came hard and often. Climax after climax, I took it all. It was my reward and punishment all in one. I deserved it and yet I had no rights to ask for it, so I would take what she would give me and hope that it would never end.  I drank until her body grew limp. I held her in my arms and allowed her to rest. I placed her in the stool located on the opposite side of the center island that we had just violated. She smiled as I wiped down the countertop, made our plates and delivered the prepared food she had just finished cooking before my invasion.

We ate breakfast staring into each other eyes. No words were spoken. She just smiled a smile that resembled the old Yazz. I knew she was still in there somewhere underneath the pain and hardness. She sometimes allowed her to come out. It was moments like this why I appreciated Yazz. She allowed herself to be vulnerable around me and I never took it for granted. We ate, and I enjoyed being satisfied with both the food she cooked and the love she fed my soul. It couldn't get any better than this I thought. Until without warning, Yazz had climbed on top of me. She had removed the apron and thong and was sitting facing me. I guess it was time for round two and I was happy to oblige. After all, I always enjoy a second helping whenever offered.

# "I Gotta Man"

**- Eve**

## Monica

We were all gathered at the dining room table at Anika and Que's house when I could not hold back the excitement. I flashed the ring; a 2-carat marquise cut diamond. It was beautiful. It was the best thing any nigga ever gave me. And trust, I have had my share of gifts from dudes in my past. Mario sat there as Que and Jay gave him dap.

"Nigga, word son, Word!" Que spoke as he got up from the table to give Mario some brotherly love. "Nigga, I asked you was something going on between yall a few times before. Secret asses have been creeping'!" Que joked, and we all laughed.

"Yo, son, that's what's up to Mario! Put a ring on that shit and claim what's your son!" Jay chimed in as they all embraced. Anika and Yazz had moved closer to get a better look. They were all smiles for us. I was so happy, and even more so that I could share this moment with my girls. The only one missing was Ayanna. It was times like this when I missed that bitch the most. But I know that she is smiling down on me; on all of us.

I was surrounded by all the people I cared about I thought as I held one of the twins and Yazz held the other. They were adorable. They smelled like pure joy and had me thinking that maybe one day this could be me. Living in a big as a house with servants and shit caring for my babies. It seemed like even being engaged again was just a dream. Had me thinking about the first time I gave my heart to someone. Reggie was my first everything. He was my first boyfriend, first kiss, the first person I had sex with and yes, the first person I loved. Reggie was three years older than me. We were high school sweethearts. I was a freshman when we met. I would cheer him on at the football and basketball games, I wore his class ring, jersey and letterman jacket. Everyone knew he was my man and I was his girl, we did everything together. If there was a party, I was there with him. He would pick me up in his Mustang blue 5.0. Girls from other schools would try to press up on him, but they were no competition for me, my curves, hips, and lips.

It wasn't until Reggie went away to college that things started to go downhill. Everyone warned me that he would find someone else or that he would outgrow me, but I knew better. I knew what we had was special or, so I thought. I remember like it was yesterday when I went to visit him on the campus of Alfred State University. I was so excited to be going up there by myself. I thought me and Reggie could use some alone time. Everything was going well. I met his suitemates and members of his football team. I felt like a superstar. Everyone seemed to know already who I was. Reggie must have been talking me up letting everyone know that I was his girl. Little did I know, there happen to be a party the same night I arrived. I had packed an outfit for every occasion, so I was ready to party.

I was cute. I had on a pair of suede brown mini shorts that zipped on the side. I had on a cream tank top and the matching brown suede crop jacket to the shorts. I wore a pair of fishnet tights and brown bootie shoes. I put my hair in a sleek ponytail with a pair or gold door knocker earrings. I looked fresh to def, and I knew it because all his suitemates looked at me when I stepped out of Reggie's room and entered the common area. As far as I was concerned, I was the baddest bitch on campus, and I was going to let everyone know.

The party was hype. The DJ had the crowd dancing and punch was laced with alcohol. It was my first college party. Reggie and I danced, and I met a few more of his friends. Reggie asked one of his friends to keep an eye on me for a few minutes. I was cool with that, plus Big Fred was crazy cool. Big Fred was cute too. I thought next time I visit; Imma has to bring one of my girls for him to mack on. Big Fred and I danced for a while. He was a good dancer, he knew how to rock with my moves, but I was careful not to put it on him, I didn't want to start some shit with him and Reggie. Big Fred even kept my solo red cup filled. I was having so much fun that I did not notice that it had been 45 min later. I asked Big Fred if he knew where Reggie went. He smiled and tried to assure me that he would be back shortly. Somehow, I did not buy that, but I played it cool. I whispered in Big Fred's ear if he could show me where the bathroom was. He took my hand and led me upstairs. He said he wasn't sure exactly, but he was sure it was upstairs. We opened door after door in the house laughing at the shit we saw inside each door being opened. It was like a game of hiding and seek, but we were looking for the bathroom. That was until we opened the next door.

When the door opened, I could not believe my eyes. There were Reggie and two other girls. His pants were down, and both of them were performing a blow job on him. They were naked, and the room smelled like stale sex. He yelled "CLOSE THE FUCKING DOOR!" before he noticed that I was standing in the doorway. He stumbled as he tried to pull up his jeans and come after me, but it was too late. I had run down the stairs and out the door. With tears streaming down my face, I could feel my heart beating and the pain of what just happened to smother me. I could not catch my breath. I could hear Reggie calling for me, but it was too late. How could he hurt me? How could he cheat on me? I was confused and lost. I was on campus all by myself and had no idea what to do. Big Fred had managed to catch up to me. He apologized for what just happen. "NIGGA YOU THINK I'M STUPID? YO ASS WAS COVERING FOR HIM. YOU KNEW WHERE HE WAS AND WHO HE WAS WITH. YOU THINK I'M SOME DUMB ASS BITCH?" I yelled checking him.

"Ok Monica, you right. I knew. That muthafucka doesn't deserve you. He claimed he loved you but that ain't how you treat a fine ass chick like you. You deserve a better lady." Big Fred said with confidence. "Let me get you back to the dorm," he added.

"I just wanna get the fuck out of here," I said wiping the tears off my face with the tissue Big Fred gave me.

"OK, I'll take you back to the dorm, and you can get your shit, and I'll take you home. I promise" Big Fred said.

We walked in silence back to the dorm. I packed up my belongings and sat in the common area waiting for Big Fred to come out of his room. I grew impatient waiting for Big Fred to hurry up. I stumped off to knock his door when it flew open. Fred was in the middle of changing his clothes. He had taken off his party attire and had put a sweatshirt on and was in the process of putting on his sweatpants when I barged in.

"DAMN! Big Fred." I said as I got to see the size of his manhood.

"MONICA CLOSE THE DOOR AND GET OUT!" he yelled turning away from my view.

"No!" I smiled refusing his request for privacy.

I was so upset that Reggie would cheat on me. I wanted revenge. And this opportunity was too easy to pass up. Big Fred was sure to give me what I needed and the revenge Reggie deserved.

"Naw Big Fred. Don't hide it now. I already saw what you were working with, besides you owe me." I said moving closer to Big Fred.

"YO shorty, this ain't right. You my man's girl. You mad right now, but yall will work it out. Let me just get my pants on so I can take you home." Fred spoke nervously.

"You just said I deserve better; you could be better, you sho' nuff' bigger. Don't be nervous" I said pulling on his pants and grabbing his manhood. I massaged him as he tried to pull away. I knew I could get him hard; I felt him getting excited when I backed up against him when we danced. But I had no idea it was like this. Why would I, I mean just minutes earlier I was with Reggie, but his cheating ass had been lying to me and who knows how many bitches he been fuckin'. As far as I know, this wasn't the first time. He was way too comfortable leaving me with his boy to handle his business.

I moved closer to Big Fred and grabbed his dick. It was thick and long. It was way bigger than

Reggie's. I want to know what it felt like. I wanted to know what it was like to be with someone other than Reggie. Plus, it was perfect revenge. I would show Reggie's ass how it felt.

Before Big Fred could even say something or push me away, my mouth was already around his dick. He was tall dark and handsome. I could tell by his muscular build that he could play football. He was toned, and I could feel his abs contract as I ran my fingers across his midsection. He moaned as I moved my head back and forth creating twist and turns with my tongue. I released him from my grip so I could massage him with my hand. My hand game was just as god as my blow job technique. I sucked the tip of his massive dick as my hand gilded up and down his length. I spit a little on his dick and slowly let the spit drip from my tongue onto him; I could tell it drove him crazy. I stood there working him as he let me have my way with him.

"Monica you sure this is what you wanna do?" he whispered at me.

"I'm sure Fred, I would not be here if I wasn't," I replied.

And that was all he needed to hear because Fred went all in. He helped me unzip my shorts and take off my tank top and jacket. I was wearing a black lace bra and G-string panty set. He took one look at me and smiled.

"I don't know how that fool could mess this up. You're the finest girl I've ever seen." Fred whispered in my ear.

"Show me, Fred. Show me just how fine you think I am." I whispered back.

Fred had gently placed his fingers in between my legs. I was already wet and anticipating his hard dick inside me. If his fingers were any indication of what I was in store for, it would be an experience I would never regret.

Fred picked me up and paced me on the long twin size bed. He opened my legs and kissed his way up my thighs and into my open pussy. His tongue was met with a tidal wave of wetness. It was beautiful the way he ate me. He was a gentle giant eager to please me. The way his fingers moved in and out of me and the way he licked my pussy had me arching and twisting with excitement. My reaction to Fred was all new to me. Reggie was my first, and I had nothing to compare him too. But Fred had my body moving in ways I had not yet experienced. It was foreign, and I loved it. When he was ready, he entered me.

I grunted from the massive size of his dick as it spread my lips open and I took all of him in. I could feel him touching parts of my inside that I had never felt before. My body shook from the excitement, and I can't count how many times I came all over his dick in the first few minutes for our encounter. It was everything. He stroked me long and hard, and I bucked back with every stroke. I could tell that he was impressed at my ability to take him all and to fuck him back. He kissed me, and his lips were soft. He looked at me like he had won a prize at the carnival. He was enjoying his prize, and I was happy to be claimed.

It was my time to show Big Fred just how lucky he was to be with me. I climbed every inch of his six foot three frame and planted myself on top of his dick. It stood at attention as I mounted myself and began to ride slowly. The sensation was so overwhelming. His dick must have been just as long and thick as him. I could squat and ride him; I could go all the way up and down and ride him. I even turned around and rode him from the back. He held me tight and allowed me to enjoy myself as he bucked back and I fucked him. I laid on top of him and rode him, and his dick stayed hard like steel. He cuffed my ass and rammed me into him. We both moaned and moaned as our sweaty bodies collided as we fucked each other in too many positions to count. We must have been making a lot of noise because we did not hear anyone else enter into the common area of the suite let alone the knocks at the door. Big Fred was giving me what I needed, and in return, I fucked him for his generosity. We were only interrupted by the sound of embarrassment with the scream Reggie let out when he walked in on us. He sounded like a little bitch. I turned and smiled and asked him to close the door as I continued to ride Fred until we both exploded from the sweet agony of defeat and revenge. We both laughed at what we had done and the fact that we are gotten busted.

When we were all done Fred, and I showered and got dressed. He gave me a sweatshirt to put on which fit me like a dress. We existed the dorm room and was greeted by applause as the rest of his roommates cheered us on. I guess the sounds from my moans and the grunts from Big Fred was all the entertainment the team needed. There was no sign of Reggie, which was good because deep down in my heart, I was still crying and I did not want my feelings to get in the way of one of the best sexual experiences I've had. Big Fred grabbed my bag, my hand and led me out the dorm. We walked to his car. He opened the door for me, placed my belongings in the car, and we made the two-hour trip back to Buffalo.

My relationship with Reggie taught me a lot about this world. One was you can't trust a nigga that's not in your sightline. Another was there is too much dick out here to be tied to only one man. And I never wanted to feel that way again. Reggie was my everything, I trusted him, and he betrayed me. He broke my heart, and I vowed that that shit would never happen again. Ever! But Mario was different. He knew all my dirt. He never asked questions he didn't want to know the answer to, he trusted me, and I trusted him. He was my friend and one hell of a lover. He understood me when no one else did.

And most importantly he loved me. The good, bad and ugly of me, that man loves me. And I love him. Mario would love me regardless of my faults. Being his wife would be the best thing ever. I had found my Big Fred, and this time I would not let him go.

# "Your Eyes"

**- Xscape**

## Anika

I can't believe that the wedding is less than one week away. These past two months have gone by so quickly. There wasn't must to do. Que had taken care of the venue, the flowers, and the reception. The only thing that I needed to do was get my dress and get my girls ready for the big day. Que had even secured a big name makeup and hair artist from New York City to come up and do my makeup and take care of the bridesmaids. The photographer was booked. They only thing now was to count down the days until I said I do. I was more than excited; I just could not believe that this day was finally going to happen. It seemed like, just yesterday, Que and I were kids, and he was teasing me on the playground at my uncle's house, where he would pull my ponytail or try to crack jokes about me. I knew even then that he liked me. My grandmother would say the boy that always picked on you was the one that usually had the biggest crush on you. There were times Que would hurt my feelings, and I would run crying into the house; there were other times that I could recall him picking and giving me a handful of purple, yellow and pink flowers. And now, after all these years, tears, and surprises, I would become Mrs. Quincy Lamont Thomas.

I was able to find the perfect wedding dress. Since the ceremony was an after 5 pm formal event, I was sure this dress would be a show stopper. It was a moonlight blush color and had a strapless sweetheart neckline. The dress hugged my curves in all the right places. You could barely tell I had just given birth to twins less than 2 months ago. The dress in a true mermaid style flared out into dramatic layers of tulle. The bodice was embroidered in crystals and beads that mimicked the crown jewels of the royal family. It was stunning, and I looked beautiful in it. The dress would be topped off with a train that was lined with sparkling crystals that reminded me of the diamond ring Que paced on the finger before I left the hospital with our twins. My wedding attire was all set. My bridesmaids would all be wearing strapless black satin mermaid style dresses. Que said that he was taking care of the groomsmen's attire so I guess the Devereaux Thomas wedding was set.

There were a few minor things that I wanted to take care of. I wanted to pick up a gift for Que and the twins. I Wasn't sure what to get the man that has everything and never wants for anything. Que had already taken care of so much; I just wanted to do something special for him. Since leaving the hospital, Que made sure that I had everything I needed. From the big spacious house, we lived in that he had decorated to suit my style, we had a maid, and a nanny, the cars and the money were also an added plus. He spoiled me and the twins. It would be great If I could do something unexpected for him. The question is what? I had asked Jay for suggestions. I knew the only other person that knows Que better than I would be Jay. They were truly like brothers. We were fortunate to have Jay as the Godfather of the twins. It was a testament to how Que felt about him, entrusting him with the lives of his sons was huge. So I knew that I could get some good ideas from Jay.

Jay agreed to meet me at the Cigar shop on Elmwood. According to Jay, Que had acquired a nice size cigar collection that he only smoked rare occasions. At the birth of the twins, he sent out a box of his favorite cigar to everyone under the FAM announcing the arrival of the princes of the kingdom. On certain FAM occasions Que would pull out the top-notch cigars as a goodwill gesture, so I was excited to add to his collection. I pulled into the parking lot and was greeted by Jay who was already there. He opened my door and in we went. The masculine smell of tobacco always reminded me of my visits to North Carolina as a child. Even though I never took up the art of smoking, I was familiar with the smell and the accessories needed to enjoy a good puff. Jay was busy talking to the store clerk and must have said something important because before I knew what was happening, a secret door opened up. The older store clerk smiled and said, "this was Ms. Devereaux" as he pointed me in the direction of the hidden passage. The aroma and the coolness of the room alerted me to the quality of the cigars that lined the room. It was impressive. The older gentleman began to explain the various origins of the cigars and the various tobacco qualities. I was overwhelmed and looked to Jay for his recommendation.

Jay recommends a few cigars that Que had favored in the past, so I purchased those. But, I wanted something different, unexpected, and original. The clerk suggested to have their

Torcedor hand craft a special blend cigar and present it to Que at the reception. He suggested that we do a cigar station with the special blend cigars as a gift to our guest and Que. I was delighted at the offer and thought what a wonderful surprise for Que. I agreed and made sure that Jay took care of the details of the cigar station and making sure it became a part of the reception without Que finding out. This was a mission accomplished, and I was sure Que would enjoy his surprise.

As the week went on, the excitement heightened. I and the bridesmaids had brunch, and I had given them a few thank you gifts. Because Que and I wanted everything to go off without a hitch, we had paid for everything including the bridesmaid dresses. My gift to them today included the jewelry they would be wearing the day of the wedding. The gift included a half carat, single pendant necklace that hung on a sterling silver 18-inch box chain. There were matching diamond earrings, with a tennis bracelet that had a total weight of one carat in diamonds. All the jewelry was custom ordered at King of Diamonds and came wrapped in a black velvet box with each of the bridesmaid's name and the wedding date engraved on it. I wanted to make sure that all eight of the bridesmaids had something meaningful to remember the wedding by. They were completely in awe of the gift as the each began playing with their sparkly new toys.

It was now the night before the wedding. I had decided that I would do a sleepover with the bridesmaids and a few close friends at my house. It would be the last night I would be a single woman. Come tomorrow, by the end of the day; I would be Mrs. Thomas and living the dream I had always wanted. But, tonight, I needed a little girl time. Yazz and Monica had taken over the plans for the sleepover. I just hope they didn't take it too far. Wait, what do I think of course they would take it too far. That's just what Monica and Yazz do and being I'm the first of us to tie the knot, I just know these bitches were about to cut loose and go crazy tonight. All I know was that whatever was about to go down better not interfere with me walking down the aisle.

# "Quiet Storm"

- Mobb Deep ft. Lil Kim

**Que**

It was the day of the wedding. A part of me wants to relax and embrace the day and all the excitement that was about to be bestowed upon me. I was finally gonna get the shorty I had been lovin' on since I was a youngin. Now look at me, I'm a father and about to be a husband. Anika and my sons were my heart. I vowed to protect them with my life, and I had the resources to do so. I promised Anika better, and I would deliver. There was too much at stake now. I had the FAM to answer too, Anika and my sons to take care of, there was no room for error. So while Anika was at the house, I stayed at the hotel out by the Walden Galleria. Jay, Mario, and the crew threw me a bachelor party last night. Before it could get to wild, I excused myself. I just needed time to think. Not about me marrying Anika, but the future. There was so much that had happened.

And just because I squashed one problem didn't mean another one wouldn't raise its ugly ass head and try to bite a nigga. So, while I had time to think about business and family, I decided to get my affairs in order. I called the lawyer last night, and we agreed to finalize a few things early this morning.

The doorbell rang to the penthouse. It could only be one of two people, either it was Jay or the lawyer.  I answered the door and in walked Jay. We greeted like we always have, dabbin' each other up followed with a half hug pat on the back. Jay was my man fifty grand. I trusted this dude with my life and the life of my family. He was the Godfather to my twin boys Rockmond and Draymond, or as we called them Rocky and Dray. They were daddy's little soldiers and Jay swore to protect and serve them if something ever happened to me. And today, he was standing up by my side as I promised Anika to be the husband she deserved; the whole honor and cherish shit. I needed Jay also to be a witness to the paperwork that the lawyer was bringing over; he was the only one I trusted with this type of shit.

Right on time, the lawyer rang the doorbell and Jay was kind enough to get the door for me. Samuel Brenneman Esquire was as thorough of a lawyer I could ask for. He stood all of "5'4 with a stout physique. But for me it was never about his size, Brenneman was as shady and loyal as a lawyer could be. For a white Jewish guy, he knew the inner workings of the streets like he was an O.G. He kept the secrets, knew when and what needed to be done, and took care of business no questions asked. Plus, when I called him at 3 am in the morning all my calls were answered, hell I think he kept a suit by his bedside just in case I wanted to meet at those ungodly hours of the night. Brenneman knew that in my line of business, money never sleeps and neither did I, which meant that he didn't either. As much as I paid him for his legal services, he didn't have much of choice but to be on call 24/7.

Brenneman had drawn up the documents I needed, taking care of the provisions I requested for him too. Jay signed the documents. He said that he would be in attendance later at the wedding, and just as quickly as Sam Brenneman Esquire had arrived, he was gone. I felt a little better. At least I knew I had a contingency plan for Anika and the boys, but something just did not seem right. I had told Jay to double check the facility, make sure we had security, preferably our peeps. Just to make sure my nerves were at ease, Jay suggested that he call our friends at the police station to make sure there was nothing out there of concern about the FAM. I had Jay tell Mario to make rounds today to see what the streets were saying. I did not want any waves today; not a goddamn ripple. Nothing could go wrong and mess up the day I had planned for Anika. Everything needed to be perfect or damn near there. Maybe I would feel better after they report in, but for now, I'd stay on high alert until I'm proven wrong.

It was show time. All the groomsmen were present and accounted for. We all looked fresh to def, pimped out in our black Hugo Boss tuxedos. The guys all wore black bow ties with baby pink rose boutonnieres. I wore a baby pink bow tie; I was told that the color matched Anika's dress. So yes, for Anika I would wear the pink... just this once. I'd do anything to see her smile. I had one more round of shots with my crew then it was time to roll. The guest were all seated, and the music was playing which signaled the start of the ceremony. I walked out of the side room of the Salvatore's Garden. We had rented out the entire place for the night. The ceremony would be in one room, and we reserved adjoining rooms for the reception. The other four rooms were themed rooms set up for the after reception parties. Salvatore's Garden was in for a treat. They ain't never seen black folks partyn' like we were about to get it in tonight, and our guest was in for a wedding they would never forget.

All the groomsmen were lined up front and center. Each of the Bridesmaids had made their way down the aisle; they were carrying a bouquet of blush, cream, black, and pink roses. The ladies all looked nice, but I was waiting for the main event. As the last bridesmaid made her way to the front of the floral arches that were dimly lit to resemble a summer garden at night, just as smoothly as the ladies came down the aisle, the music changed, and the doors to the banquet room opened. There Anika stood. She was the most beautiful thing I had ever seen. She looked angelic and radiant. Watching her float down the aisle took my breath away. Her dress was a moonlight pink tone that complimented her complexion. Anika glowed as her makeup accentuated her natural beauty. But that dress and Anika's figure in it was the centerpiece of the event. The dress hugged every curve on her body, it was as close to heaven and the angels that I was ever going to get, and she was all mines. The sparkles in her dress caught the light in the room and set off a burst of lights in a rainbow of colors that cascaded throughout the room. It was amazing. Anika looked amazing. If I wasn't in love with her before, watching her walk towards me made me fall in love with her all over again.

The tears in my eyes never fell, but I knew how wonderful the feeling was when Anika said, "I do." It was official, and with all 400 people in attendance I placed the 4-carat pear-shaped diamond on her finger and kissed my bride. Thunderous applause filled the room. We kissed long and hard, and when we stopped, I found myself mesmerized by her beauty. She was everything I had hoped for, and today she made me the luckiest man on earth. Damn, how did I get so lucky? I thought to myself as we jumped the decorated broom as a symbol of our union. With Anika in my arms, I carried her away to a private room so that I could have her to myself for just a moment. She was all smiles as her many admirers cheered and greeted us. I was finally alone with my stunning bride. While we were taking a moment to ourselves, our guest was being treated to a cocktail hour that resembled the Las Vegas strip, and, there were many buffet stations offering every delicacy anyone could crave for.

I just needed a moment to look at Anika before I shared her with our guest. She had taken my breath away and looking at her made me love her even more. She was the mother of my sons and the only person I knew truly loved me; the good, the bad, and the ugly. She knew what I was about, and no matter how hard things got between us, we always found our way back to each other. But this time there was nothing that was going to separate us. I would always be right here. I would always protect, love, honor and live for her. Her smile lit up the room as the photographer took a few photo shots of us. I could not take my eyes off of her. This was one of the few times that I allowed myself to be vulnerable and live in the moment. Smile after smile and shot after shot, Anika and I posed for the photographer. We even took a few candid's with the twins. Everything about her in this moment was magical. The way she handled my sons, the way she seemed to just bring calm to my chaotic world was nothing short of a miracle. I watched with admiration as the woman that I loved, and the mother of my twins took control of us, and lovingly owned the night.

I wanted Anika to be the first to see the Reception Hall. Since we were being married in winter, I wanted to create a winter wonderland. The whole room, thanks to the help of the wedding planner, was done up in winter white, crystals, and gold. There was white satin draped on the walls, and gold accents throughout the room. White linen covered the tables that were decorated with calla lilies, roses, and hydrangeas, none of which are in season right now. The room had crystals draped across the ceiling along with tear drop shaped string lights; there were tall white birch branches in gold and white floor vases scattered throughout the room. There was not one area of the banquet hall that was not covered and reimagined to look like a wonderland; even the dance floor was covered in special lighting that showcased our initials on the floor. I could tell by the look on Anika's face that she was pleased with what I had done. All the white and the special lighting made Anika's dress glow; it was something out of a fairy tale. I was her King, and she was my Queen. We were the two that were destined to be together, but the odds always stacked against us. And now, all that has changed, hopefully for the better.

# "The Most Beautifullest Thing In This World"

**- Keith Murray**

## The Reception

## Yazz

Anika looked amazing. I was so happy for my girl and Que. Que out did himself. This reception was off the hook; he spared no expense. The food was good excellent, not your ordinary banquet cuisine. Que had chefs from all over flown in to recreate some of his and Anika's favorite dishes. It was a delight to the pallet. I had never seen so many options and choices; I could tell all 400 guests felt the same. It was a white glove experience I knew a lot of these niggas had never known, but so far everyone was behaving themselves. I'm sure Mario laid down the rules for tonight. Besides, if you were important enough to get the invitation, you already knew what was expected. So there was no reason to worry, we were all surrounded by family, close friends, and associates of the FAM. This was the biggest event to hit the streets of Buffalo, NY since Rick James came on the scene.

I had never seen so many high profile individuals in one place. That's how you know The FAM was the shit. This wedding was the hottest ticket in town, and I heard that the after party was going to be even better. I couldn't wait to see what other surprises Que had planned throughout the night for Anika and their guest. All this love shit had me feeling some kind of way. Jay was lookin' good as fuck in that tux. I could see Jay eyein' me, so I knew he was feeling the same energy I was. This dress had me showing all my curves and fit like a glove. Yeah, there would be a lot of niggas gettin head tonight, Jay and I wouldn't be the only ones fuckin' tonight.

## Mario

Damn! My man did his thing. This wedding was off the chain, goes to show what real money can buy. Monica better gets no ideas, cause our wedding will not be like this shit here. Que was the top dog; his pocket was way deeper than my shit, there would be no competition. I was happy for Que and Anika. Hell, I was happy for Monica and me. Just being around black love like this when you a street nigga gave me hope. Hope that a nigga like me can have a future instead of living for today only; having a future a family and a wife.

All this mushy shit was over the top though. Their first dance was cute. My nigga Que looked relaxed for once; lord knows he never took a break from thinking. I guess that's what happens when you sit on top. If the streets don't sleep than you don't either. But we had the building on lock, wasn't nothing going down without us knowing first. Wait, what am I thinking, ain't nothing going down today but this party right here. Strapped or not, not a nigga alive would try us today. And I'll drink to that, as I raised my glass to one of the many toasts that were given in honor to Que and Anika.

I was happy to see that Auntie Rose was able to attend the wedding. All the heads of the board were present and accounted for. It was a beautiful thing knowing that they blessed this union. I think that if Anika and Que had just asked in the beginning, we could have avoided a lot of bullshit, but they together now and that's all that matters now. "To the King and his Queen," we all raised our glasses again and toasted to the bride and groom. "Black love may it reign forever," cheers as I took another sip of champagne.

## Monica

"Yo, this wedding is da bomb," Que knows how to do it big. Everything was like something out of one of those bridal books. Anika was the luckiest girl in the world, that nigga was going to spoil her rotten. As if she stuck up ass needed any other excuses, I thought jokingly. Naw for real, I was happy for both of them. And hell, I was next. I could not wait for me and Mario to do it up like this. You just wait, our wedding was going to be the shit. Every bitch in my bridal party better be snatched, 'cause there won't be no out of checked bodies in my wedding pictures. If you ain't got no hair, you better get a weave; no ass get a butt lift no titties buy that push-up bra. I wanted bad body bitches representing me on my big day, 'cause Imma bad body bitch.

The DJ was on point; he had all of us on the dance floor. Old and young, from the electric slide to the butterfly, hustle and the tootsie roll we were all getting it in. Song after song we partied and that was just the beginning. They opened up the specialty bars for unlimited flow. There was a vodka bar and a Martini Bar. Each had a signature drink created in honor of the Bride and Groom. I was in heaven. Anika had surprised Que with a Cigar station. Niggas were puffin like we were in Cuba. They had a desert station complete with Anika's favorite ice creams and candies. Que left nothing to be desired. He covered everything Anika and the guest could want. From the music to the food, to the other indulgences, it was pure sin for a heavenly union.

Mario had found me on the dance floor. He stayed on me like glue. It felt good knowing that he had eyes only for me. We rocked to the music like we were making love in the privacy of my house. I could feel his dick imprint pressing through those tuxedo pants. It would have gotten my panties wet, but I wasn't wearing any. My dress was so damn tight; I didn't want this fat ass to be walking down the aisle with a panty line.

The dress didn't stop me from getting it in though; I was just cute about it. We were all on the dance floor, Anika and Que were in the middle of the sea of onlookers. It was their day, and they deserved all the support and love they would get. This truly was the party of the year and this time next year; it would be my time I thought as we all cheered Que and Anika on as they dances and enjoyed their day.

## Jay

I was happy for my brother and sister. Que had loved Anika for as long as I could remember. It was good to see that this life we lead could provide moments of calm and happiness. We all know that mostly isn't the case. I was happy to stand up and be the best man, wouldn't have had it any other way. Whatever Que needed I had his back, no matter what. Just to make sure things went uneventful, I made sure that security was tight. Made my rounds throughout the facility doing check in with everyone. I made sure that the board members of the FAM were comfortable. I kept the drinks flowing and made sure the party continued as planned. It was Que's ask of me, and I wanted him to relax and enjoy this moment because it would be business, as usual, tomorrow, he could worry then. Tonight he needed to focus on his bride and the future that lay ahead of them.

When Yazz walked down that aisle, she looked stunning. The smile on her face gave me all I needed to feel complete. That dress, her hair and makeup already showed what I've known since we met, Yazz was truly a diamond among rocks. Everything about her shined brightly, despite what she had been through. She came through that hell stronger. Her battle wounds she wore like a badge of honor. I had come to understand that transformation was never about me, but her acceptance of who she wanted to be. She had been running for so long form so much that she didn't have time to just be herself. The situation in Michigan as unfortunate as it was, gave birth to the real Yazz, someone who is confident, strong, intelligent and deadly. She wore all those traits now, and it was the biggest turn on. It enhanced her sex appeal and drove me even more crazy. Dancing with her had m,e on 100. I wanted her, I needed her, and one day when she was ready, I knew we could have this too. A family; a life outside of the FAM; a happy ever after.

Just when the guest thought the celebration couldn't get any better, the other banquet rooms were opened up. Each room had been transformed into a nightclub setting. To add to the excitement, Que had top performers flown in to give a personal concert to his new bride. There was a new group called Jagged Edge that graced the stage and perform some of their new hits. They were one of Anika favorite groups at the moment. The crowd rocked back and forth singing along. They did three of their songs before leaving the stage. On their last song, they called the bride and groomed up on stage. They sang "Promise" as Que and Anika danced for the crowd. It was a real playa move. Donnell Jones, 702, and Q-tip all took to the stage to congratulate the happy couple and perform one or two songs. The party was just getting started. The liquored flowed, the cigars stayed rolled, and for once in my life, it felt good to be on the winning team. "Cheers to the Que and Anika" Q-tip said as he started singing Vibrant Thing," CHEERS!! we all screamed and started singing along.

The after party was about to pop off and it was barely 11:30 pm. I thought it was a good time to make my rounds again, this time Yazz decided to join me. The guest was all enjoying themselves. There was even a VIP area for the elite guest. We checked on them first. Auntie Rose, Uncle Clio, Sargent, Auntie Bonnetta, Mac, and Cousin Matt among others were all in attendance. It was the first time that I've seen them all together outside of FAM business. Everyone was all smiles and seemed relaxed, enjoying the festivities. I made sure the drinks kept coming to the VIP area, and that fresh hors-d'oeuvres were brought over for the guest.

Everything seemed to be going well. I had visited the check-in spots, spoke with security, and even walked the perimeter with Yazz. All was good. Yazz and I made our way back into Salvatore's Italian Gardens. I took this time to let Yazz know how I was feeling. The moment was so right, the atmosphere had set the tone, and after witnessing Que and Anika make it happen, I couldn't imagine not having Yazz in my life. She was so beautiful. And, the sacrifices she had made, showed me just how dedicated and in love with me she was. I grabbed her hand as we walked the long hallway. I sat her down and began to express my love for her. She blushed, and for a moment I was able to see a glimpse of the old Yazz peek through. Her eyes always showed me the softer side of her, and at this moment, I drowned in their reflection.

I went to reach for my pocket when I heard the door being yanked open. My trance was broken by the look on the face of the two soldiers that were guarding the perimeter of the building. Something was wrong. Just then another door opened. It was the members of the board for the FAM. "Awe Shit," I said out loud as I immediately ran toward the Board. It was serious, and I knew it. Just then, door after door opened and soldiers were rushing in from all directions. The alarm had been sounded. Shit was about to go down, and we were all at risk.

# "Banned from TV"

**- N.O.R.E.**

**The After Party**

**Jay**

"FUCK!!!" I screamed. "Ok, Yazz gets the Board to the back of the building. We have a few cars back there waiting. Split up, no more than three individuals to a car, this way if one car gets stop they don't get us all. Go now!" I said with urgency.

Uncle Clio stayed behind to help out. I had him find Que and Anika and get them out to safety. Just then, Mario came running out of the main banquet hall. I gave him the burner and told him to "get to the front line. Hold them back as long as you and the team can. I'll leave one car for you to get to, be there in ten minutes. Stick to the plan, don't deviate". We dabbed up and off Mario ran. "FUCK!" I screamed out. I know we had a plan in place, we always prepared for the what if, but I never thought that we would have our backs against the wall like this.

"Goddamnit, the Feds were coming and in full force. Our informants in the police department just got the news and alerted us as soon as they could. With an estimated arrival time of fifteen minutes, we had no time to lose. The Board's inside people must have given them the same info. "Stick to the plan" I reminded myself. Not one nigga on this team wasn't born, raised and ready for this moment. The real enemy of our way of life was never another crew, but the government, and with a RICO charge coming down we all stood to lose everything. There was no way this shit was happening on my watch, not under Que's reign. "FUCK!" I screamed as I headed into the banquet hall in search for Que.

## Yazz

I got the members of the Board into the cars as Jay had instructed. They were headed straight to the airport, no stopping. There were two private chartered jets waiting. They would take one, and the other was reserved for Que, Anika, the twins, Mario, Monica and me. Aunt Rose was hard headed. Everyone one else got in the cars and understood the plan, but not her. She refused to stick to the plan. I could not convince her to get in the car. She stated that she would be best served if she stayed behind, just in case she said. Just in case what I asked? She just rolled her eyes and stood her ground. Fuck it, I did not have the time to argue; I needed to get everyone to safety. Next, I needed to find Monica and Anika and get her and the twins out of here. Auntie Rose would just have to come along. I kicked off my heels and jetted down the hallways back toward the main banquet hall. Monica was coming out of the room. I knew she had figured out that something was going on. I asked her where were Anika and the twins. She said her mother had left with the twins about an hour ago. That was the best news I had heard all night. Anika had gone to change into another dress to get ready to leave with Que, Monica confessed with a confused look…

"What is going on Yazz" Monica asked?

"Our worst nightmare" I replied.

I knew she understood what I meant by my reply. We were off to grab Anika and get the hell out of here.

## Mario

It was almost showtime. The FAM ran deep and today was no exception to the rule. We had about 200 plus niggas on site. I even called in for back up. They may not get here until the fireworks begin, but at least the blue would get it from the front and back. Everything was set on my end; I had positioned crew all over the grounds. We looked like an army ready to go to war. If the world did not know who the fuck the FAM was, tonight might be their first introduction to some real thug nigga shit. I had about five minutes to get back to the back of the building. I just needed to remind everyone what was at stake and more importantly why we do what we do. We ride or die for the FAM. Not just when the game and money is good, but especially when opposition comes up against us. Now was one of those time. We needed to stand our ground and protect what was ours to the death. From the looks on their faces, they were all in agreeance. The time was now, and we needed to deliver.


## Que

Jay had just informed me of what was going on. I knew it, I fuckin knew it. I could feel it in my bones that something was off. As we were talking in walked my lawyer. Brenneman must have gotten word of what was about to go down. He came to warn me to get the hell out of here, but it was too late. I had already changed into a pair of jeans and a tee. Not what I was going to wear to go away with my bride, but something comfortable for battle. Yeah, we had a plan in place as a precaution, but NO ONE needed to die for me. I could take whatever heat was coming my way. I did not need to put my wife, sons or my people in any unnecessary harm. Even my plan had a contingency plan. It was time I let Jay and my lawyer in on what was going to happen next.

"Are we all clear on how this is going to go down?" I asked Jay and Brenneman. We shook on it. I had Brenneman give instructions to the DJ.

From there, we would meet up at his office. Brenneman left to take care of his task. Jay, I could tell did not agree with the plan, but I knew he knew it made the most sense. It was also the right thing to do. I had a family to think about and a business that depended on me making the right moves, and this was the right move. Jay took off to find Mario. We had less than five minutes to get the hell out of here. I needed to make sure Anika was ok, and she understood what was about to happen. She was the only one, other than Jay and Mario, I knew would not like this plan. I needed her to understand that I meant every word I said to her today. I would never leave her and that my word was bond; I would never put her in harm's way. Those were promises that I needed to keep, and this pan allowed me to make sure everyone made it out of here alive, and I could have my happily ever after with Anika.

# "Hate Me Now"

- Nas

## Mario

Jay and I got word the ladies had made it out safely. We were just waiting for Que to get his ass in the car. This nigga had changed up the game. I was ready for some action, and so were the soldiers that stood behind me. If it meant no one had to die, and a few fewer mothers bury sons today, then so be it. But that Nigga needs to know we all would take a bullet for him and the FAM.

The crowd from the reception existed the building as the DJ informed everyone that the reception had come to a close. Oblivious of the chaos that was about to reign down on us all, the guest left smiling and reliving their favorite parts of the event. Up till this moment, it was the event of the century. Shiiid, if we make it out of this, it will go down as the event that defined the FAM. And being able to avoid the Fed's would just add to the legend that we were already bigger than life. Finally, Que shows up. He was trying not to bring attention to us, but guest wanted to talk to hm as they were leaving. He finally makes it to the car and not a moment to spare; you could see the flashing lights for what looked like a mile long parade of police cars coming directly at us from both directions. It was time to break the fuck out. Either way, the road would be tricky, and there was no guarantee we would make it out of this alive, but this plan at least made way for everyone else to get away safely.

We pulled out, and the tires screeched. We heard the sound of the fireworks that Que had ordered being set off. It was the perfect ending to a wonderful night and the perfect distraction for our getaway. We pulled out onto Transit Road. We took a hard right toward Highway 33; it was the easiest way to get downtown. We knew they would be on us with the quickness, but it was a straight shot to the lawyer's office. With his foot on the peddle Jay hit the gas and the race began.

It was like they anticipated us making a move. As soon as we made our way past the first cop car, it was like we were leading a caravan the way they all turned and started following us. Local police tried to interfere, but they were no match for us. I swear Jay was like a professional race car driver. He could whip the shit out of a car or truck. Today, he was putting his talent to use. We made it onto Highway 33, and the quest was on, doing speeds of 100 plus, weaving in and out of what traffic was on the highway. We had a team of police, troopers and federal agents following us. What we didn't know was the roadblock they had stationed on the highway would pose a problem for us. They had rolled out the spikes, and they pierced through the tires two at a time as we rode over them. There was no way to avoid that shit. The only saving grace was the tires Jay had put his whip could go a few miles before going flat. But if you factor in the speed we were doing along with the size of the puncture holes from the spikes; we would be lucky if we lasted another two or three miles. Que got on the burner and asked for help. Whoever was not tied up at the banquet hall could easily get to the highway. The alarm was set off, and help was coming. We passed by the Eggert Avenue exit and noticed they were trying to block off the exit ramps.

No worries because we just needed niggas to be able to get on the highway. As we hit the Suffolk exit, we noticed three cars entering at high speeds... had to be soldiers of the FAM coming to help. They got behind us to slow traffic down and give us a chance to dip on these fools. We were nearing the Grider street exit, and a few more cars entered onto the highway before it got shut down.  The highway was congested enough that we had a little lead on the caravan. Just then two cars pulled up on us.  We needed to ditch the car we were in before the tires gave out. The driver on the right was a runner for the FAM; he told us to swing a hard right at the Humboldt Street exit. We needed to follow him.

Jay and Que looked at each other. I knew we would not make it. We needed to do something… fast. "Jay you need to pull over now" I spoke up.

"Mario we're almost there" Jay tried to reason.

"We need to stick to the plan" Que demanded.

"Naw Que, we won't make it. The tires damn near down to the rims, no way in hell we making it all the way to the Humboldt exit. We got to pull the car over now if you are ever gonna get out dis shit" I demanded. Both Jay and Que were looking at each other. They knew I was right; we had no choice. Jay signaled for the other car to pull over now. The driver pulled over, and Que and Jay got out.

"What the fuck you doing Mario?" Que questioned as I got out of the back seat and into the driver seat of the car.

"Nigga doesn't do this," Jay said. "We can make this shit work." he pleaded.

"No, we can't get bruh. This is the only way" I confessed. "You both know I'm right. Now get the fuck outta here before they see that you changed cars. GO MUTHAFUCKAS!!" I yelled. Jay and Que hopped into the other car and ducked down. The driver put his hazard light on, popped the trunk of the Ford Escort and got out of the car and acted like he was fixing a flat tire. It was ingenious; I thought as I quickly merged into traffic.

Once again it's on. They were closing in on me which meant that they did not notice the exchange of passengers from one vehicle to another. The tires were deflating fast, and I knew what I needed to do. At that moment I realized just how lucky I was, I had lived my life with purpose. I had been groomed to be the best street warrior and possibly a leader of sorts. I had done a lot of dirt in my time, nothing I'd regret, just somethings I would have done differently. Maybe I would have laughed a little bit more or loved a little harder. Hell, I would have left Buffalo and visited some exotic island and gotten away from these streets, if only for a moment. One thing I wish I had done was said goodbye to Monica. I know she will never forgive me for this. I also knew that she understood the life I lived and my dedication to the FAM. It was who I was and what I lived for until she came along. Monica brought peace to my world in a place where death and suffering exist. Happiness is so short term, and with Monica, I had hope for an eternity of happy days. Damn, I loved that crazy ass bitch. And I hoped she understands why I had to do what I'm about to do, the reason why she will only see me in her thoughts and dreams from this point on. And why she will always be the best thing to happen to me. It was Showtime and this time I was going to take center stage. I was going to steal some of Que and Jay's thunder; it was my time to shine and damn it I wasn't gonna be no punk about it either. It was the moment I was born for, what I was raised to do and who I was. I was a soldier for the FAM, and it was time I go to war.

# "The Symphony"

## - EPMD ft. Redman, Method Man and Lady Luck

**Jay**

"DAMNIT MARIO!!" I yelled out loud to an empty room. I could feel the tears swelling up in my eyes. "Stick to the plan, that is all we had to do," I repeated to myself. It was all over the news. Once Mario drove off, Que and I laid low in the car until all the police passed us, then the driver took us to a safe house. From there we changed clothes, made a few calls, and agreed to head down to the lawyer's office. We knew the Feds were still looking for us. So needless to say the block was hot. But all we needed to do was get to Brenneman's office on Seneca Street and allow him to take us into the police. That was the plan; no one was supposed to get hurt, that was the plan. "SHIT!!" I screamed. It was all over the news. Channel three eyewitness news had broadcasted the events live. That fucking Mario…that kid was all heart and no brains. Once the car stopped, Mario decided that going quietly was never his thing. Mario was a warrior; a trigger happy nigga; no retreat no surrender type of nigga. He was about that life and was quick to let a muthafucka know it too. But over the past few months, he had shown some maturity, a calmness about himself. I guess that's what love will do to you. I don't know why I'm surprised but not surprised that Mario opened fire on the police. Once he started shooting, it was over. They fired back, and before I could even turn away from the TV, Mario lay dead in the center lane of the Kensington Highway, right at the Jefferson Street exit. That shit broke my heart. Mario was like my younger brother; we were a family. I had his back and he damn sure had mines. If Mario could have just stuck to the plan, but I know he couldn't, it wasn't in him, and this moment, it broke my heart that I did not teach him better.

The news outlets replayed Mario's murder over and over again. With each relay, I grew more and more upset. I wanted to scream and yell or punch the shit out of something, but what good would it do, Mario wasn't going to come back.

The sadness and anger became intertwined, and my emotions were taking over. My heart hurt, Mario was like my little brother. He had been running behind Que and me since he was knee-high. I watched him go from a boy to a man, from a soldier to a warrior in these streets. I knew a part of Mario wanted to mature and do better, to know a better way of life, but when this is all you know, when slangin' and bangin' is all you have to show for your existence, how could he really accomplish anything else other than to become a deprived soul seeking glory from the barrel of a gun? Mario had so much potential; I just wish he could have lived long enough to believe in himself the way I did. I've been thinking only of myself; I could only imagine what Monica must be feeling right now. I did not know where the ladies were, if they were ok, or if they had seen the news. All I could say is that nothing in this game would prepare her for losing the man she loved like this. My heart sank just a little more from just thinking about her loss. It took me back to when all that shit went down with Yazz; I thought that someone had killed her. The pain, the sleepless nights, the constant worrying and the not knowing. If the thought of losing Yazz brought unbearable pain and agony, then Monica was sure to be in hell. Mario didn't have to go out like that, but he was a warrior for the FAM, and we could or should not expect him to be or do anything other than die by the bullet. That doesn't mean that it won't hurt; hurt like a muthafucka…

## Que

"Damnit Mario," I said grabbing my head. This dude was my little nigga, my ace, and above all he was family. I should have known. Mario was always about this life. It was what I admired about him most, but he didn't have to do this. I had told him and Jay that it didn't matter that the feds were coming for us, they ain't got shit on us; not one damn thing. When I tell you that our operation ran like a top-notch corporation, it did. I made sure that anyone sitting at the table with me understood the nature of the business, our objective, and the need for full privacy and discretion. Everything I did flow just like that. There was never any evidence, no witnesses, and above all, no paper trail. So the feds coming for us is purely on suspicion. Them assholes ain't got shit on me, let alone the FAM, and that made all this other shit was pointless.

There is no way Mario should have caught a bullet. I wanna blame Jay, but all them niggas panicked. Instead of tryna to go to war with the federal government, the minute they got word that the feds were coming, they should have cleared the building. They wasted time, valuable time trying to ante up, and for what? Nothing! Now I got my brother on the fucking news going out like some blaze of glory in the hood movie. And again, over what? Not a goddamn thing and I'll put my life on that.

Furthermore, what Mario did do was potentially put a light on the FAM when before they didn't have anything. So, if I were them, I'd be thinking why in the hell would someone we had circumstantial shit on start a shootout. What the fuck is this nigga trying to hide or protect? Niggas panicking put everybody in jeopardy: the Board, Anika and my sons, our guest and themselves. The operation of the FAM was that we always hid in plain sight and now they want to go public. This was a fight we would not win. They would have been questioning everyone at the event fishing for anything that could link us and the FAM to their RICO charges. The more I sat there in Brenneman's office thinking of the night's events, the more the anger grew in me.

So according to Brenneman's sources in the D.A.'s office, it's a RICO charge, all speculation of course, but they issued a warrant for Jay and me. Which made me even more pissed because Mario would have walked, they weren't even after him. Panicking and not sticking to the plan, now my brother, friend, and warrior were dead for nothing more than a suspicion. It was all about Jay, and I. Mario would have been home free and in a position to handle business while we handle this. Now what?  I'm sure the Board members are long gone by now. Who the fuck was going to handle business?  Brenneman told me not to worry about that right now. He seemed to be optimistic that this would blow ever in a few days.

"I'll have you out on the streets and back to business in a few days" Brenneman stated calmly. For now, I would have to trust this nigga, because I didn't have any other options and if it was only for a few days, business could survive.

You know what won't survive, me not getting in touch with my wife. In all the commotion, I forgot to get in touch with Anika. Brenneman assured me that he left specific instruction on where to take her and her friends that were with her. I knew that she was with Monica and Yazz, so I found comfort in knowing that she was with family. "Oh yeah there was and older women with them too." Brenneman declared. Older women, I thought, who the fuck could that be? Maybe it was her mom's or another family member, either way; she was in good hands. Besides the hard part of the night was over. I had married the girl of my dreams, I had promised her through good and bad times that I would always make my way back to her, just didn't think that bad day would happen so soon. But Anika knows the life well enough to know despite what they might be showing about Mario's ass on the news outlets; I would never do anything to jeopardize my life and our family. My goal now was to get back to her and the sooner, the better.

# "Incarcerated Scarfaces"

**- Raekwon**

**Que**

Together Brenneman, Jay, and I rode the few blocks in his black Lincoln town car to the federal building downtown. I had always assumed that the federal buildings were all closed up on the weekends. Not the case, at least not this one. Brenneman had called a head and let someone in the office know that he was bringing us in. We went through two stop lights then made a right turn. In between the many one ways, streets that lined downtown Buffalo stood a stark colored cement building. Brenneman drove around to the back of the building. We were greeted by two armed men at the entrance of the parking garage. We drove under the building and up to the side door that was crowded by what I could only assume were federal agents. Before unlocking the door, Brenneman spoke.

"Que, remember the plan. I'll take care of everything on the outside until you get out. I'll make sure Anika knows where you're at, and as soon as I can, I'll have her here to see you. I don't have to tell you what to do but just remember, you don't talk to them EVER without me present, understood?"

"I already know the drill, Brenneman. You just better live up to your part of this arrangement. Jay and I can handle ourselves. You make sure the women are taken care of." I replied.

I took one look at Jay, and we both knew it was game time.

"They ain't got shit on us, Jay. Stick to the plan." I reiterated.

"I know yo, I ain't even worried. We the FAM, ain't nobody got shit on us" Jay said as he smiled. We dabbed each other up as Brenneman unlocked the car doors. We opened the car doors, and agents pulled quickly pulled us out of the car.

They pulled Jay out of the back seat and me out of the front passenger seat. They had us both pinned to the car as they proceeded to handcuff us and read us our Miranda rights. I looked at Jay and he at me. It was truly game time except more than just the score was on the line, our whole way of life was at stake. I hadn't been sitting at the top of the thrown long enough for this shit to be happening. I had made a lot of promises that I needed to keep. The future of the FAM lay with me especially now that Mario was gone. I prayed in a few days everything would be back to business as usual, well almost.

They had escorted Jay and me into the building, Brenneman was parking the car and would be in shortly. They guided us into two separate rooms. They sat me down, and I could see Jay, we both smiled knowing the game we were about to play. He nodded, and I nodded back. They ain't got shit on us. I thought to myself as the doors closed. Let the games begin. Chess, spades or checkers, didn't matter how these federal muthafuckas came at us, we were ready to play. As Mario would say, this is what I was born for, raised to be, and who the fuck I was. Let's do this shit so I can get back to business.

# "It's All About the Benjamins"

**Puff Daddy and the Family**

## Anika

"Wait for what, Que's being held by the feds? I don't understand how this could be happening, and on all days, or wedding day" I cried as Brenneman informed me about the latter part of tonight's events. "When can I see him? When are they going to release him?" I asked as I got up off the couch to grab my coat and purse to get ready to leave.

"Anika, are you listening to what your lawyer is saying Ma? "Yazz spoke as she grabbed me. I looked her in her eyes.  "This could not be happening to me. Not know. Just a few hours ago I was the happiest bride, and now, they're trying to tell me that my husband is not coming home, that my sons won't be with their father." I broke down and cried harder.

## Aunt Rose

"Anika gets your ass up, Dupre' women have never been weak. Get off that floor right the fuck now. You may have your father's last name, but you have the tenacity, determination, and the blood of generations of women that have endured way more than what you and Que are going through. You gonna be alright. I'll see to that. But right now baby girl, you need to get yourself together. You got those boys, Que, and the whole family depending on you. You don't have time for this shit." I demanded of Anika. She had been pampered way too long. It was time she got off that high throne of hers and did the work that put her there. "Chile, you been living your whole life protected. It is time that you show this world just who you are. Que's legacy as the head of the FAM and everyone's way of life depends on you. Do you understand what I'm saying to you Chile? Look at me" I demanded.

## Anika

"Auntie Rose, I don't know the first thing about running the family business. I just can't... I mean you'll have to find someone else. I'm not cut from that cloth. I don't know the first thang about running the streets and hustling. Plus, I have the boys, I don't want them in the streets like this. I have to set the example. I just can't do it. It can't be me I said as I turned to face the window overlooking Lake Erie. We were housed in a penthouse apartment that apparently Que and I owned. It was considered safe. Being that we weren't sure of our main home was under surveillance or being searched, Brenneman thought this location was best for now until he could check things out. "Damnit Que, you promised!!" I thought to myself as the tears rolled down my face.

SLAP!!! I felt the tingling sensation across my face as Auntie Rose's hand left an imprint along my left cheek.

**Aunt Rose**

"Anika baby, there is no one else. With Mario gone, there is no one else we can trust. It is you. So you gonna have to put on your big girl panties and get it together. Besides, I know you can do this, and I won't let you fail. I'll teach you everything I know and then some. Your lawyer here, Brenneman, he'll help won't you?" I said turning to look at him. He shook his head in agreeance.

"Anika, Que gave specific instructions for me to make sure that you and the boys got all the help you needed. Whatever you do, you'll have the full support of my office and all the connections your husband has." Brenneman confided.

"You see a girl; we got you. But you gonna have to take this throne and rule even harder than anyone before you. It's the first time a woman has sat at the head of The FAM. There's going to be people questioning your ability to lead, enemies thinking now is a good time to take what is ours, and people wanting to take what's rightfully yours. But you gonna show them, I won't let you fail. And by the time you're done, you'll have taken The FAM to a whole nother level.  Now wipe those tears. Que and Jay went to be ok. You and those boys gone be just fine, we got work to do." I said as I sat down and took a sip of Hennessy.

## Anika

I looked at Aunt Rose. She was right. Now was the time for me to stand up and do this for Que, our family, and The FAM. I wiped my tears as I had been instructed. Everything Aunt Rose said was true. It was time for me to grow up; it was time for me to take charge; it was time for me to lead. I wasn't sure what that all meant, but I was confident that Aunt Rose and Brenneman would help me figure it out. I looked at Monica who had barely stopped crying; then I looked at Yazz. They were both nodding their heads in agreeance. They walked over to me, and we hugged each other. I knew with these two by my side I could and would make this work. It was all too much I thought, but I knew I had to try. Que believed that I could do this, I had to at least protect what was ours.

"Girl we got your back" Yazz added.

"You got this" Monica chimed in. "Mario would want me to help you out the same way I help Que out. I'm in," she Added.

"You already know, Jay wouldn't have it any other way. I'm down too" Yazz continued.

I guess it's final. Yazz, Monica, Brenneman, and Aunt Rose all looked toward me.

I was ready. Enough crying, there was work being done, and I was ready to make myself known. I was Mrs. Quincy Lamont Thomas, a Dupre', I came from a blood line of powerful women, I was a mother, and now I would be the head of the most powerful drug family along the eastern coast. The throne was mine, and I would not let them down.

"I'll Do It!" I said firmly. "I'm all in!

# The Author's Page

A.A.Lewis was born and raised on the Eastside of Buffalo, NY. She now lives with her husband and 2 sons in MIchigan. The 716 Back to Business is the second book in The 716 trilogy.

A.A. Lewis is currently working on a number of books that are set be release in 2019.

To contact or stay up ro date on A.A. Lewis please visit her facebook page at Author A A Lewis

https://www.facebook.com/profile.php?id=100028446872668&ref=bookmarks